Gulfside Girls

A HAVEN BEACH NOVEL

REBECCA REGNIER

One

ALI

Ali would forever refer to January 9th of that year as Crapfecta Day, due to the Trifecta of Crap that landed on her life.

She was busy. That was a given. Spinning millions of plates was her baseline of activity. Ali pinned her hopes on next month. Next month, things would be better; they would calm down, and she could get back to a manageable level of spinning plates. Whatever that was.

As the Assistant to the Events Director at the Frogtown Convention Center, Ali was used to having her hands full. She was used to making people happy, even when their demands were unreasonable. Ali prided herself on over-performing. It may not be in the contract her vendors signed, but she made it happen. Smoothly. And with a smile. She took pride in her work and her attitude about her work.

Frogtown Convention Center was the largest convention space and venue in Toledo, Ohio. It was in the center of downtown. You could walk to the ballpark and the hockey arena. There was a view of the river and easy access to the thriving local restaurants.

Frogtown was attached to the best hotel in Toledo. The convention spaces she oversaw regularly hosted festivals, trade shows, and, of course, conventions. Ali Harris planned every event down to the number of extension cords each exhibitor required.

And that was the current conundrum. The vendor in front of her was in the throes of extension cord envy.

"We need four outlets, that's why we need the corner booth. Jerry promised us the corner." Archie Hopper was hopping mad. And insistent. And loud. "T-Town Heating and Cooling is the third-largest heating and cooling company in Northwest Ohio. We have the biggest display."

The air conditioning guy was overheated. That was clear as his demands and shouting directed at her echoed throughout the giant mostly empty convention space. Archie's face was beet red, and spit shot out of his teeth right toward Ali. She stayed calm. Human freon for this moment. That was her skill. She'd de-escalate the moment and solve his problem.

And, of course, this went straight back to Jerry. Every problem at the Frogtown Convention Center led back to her boss, Jerry.

Jerry Scheck, Director of the Frogtown Convention Center, wouldn't make her Assistant Director. Like Michael Scott of *The Office*, he insisted she was the Assistant to the Director. She had all of the work, none of the pay, and, of course, not even a nicer-sounding title.

Ted, Ali's husband, continued to tell her she needed to push for the title change. He wanted her to have something that sounded prestigious, even though the job was the job. Well, that little discussion would have to wait. Jerry had created a mess, and the mess was currently yelling in her face in the form of Archie Hopper.

Ali imagined Jerry and Archie at Sylvania Country Club last summer, drinking, playing a round of golf, and hitting on the beer cart girls. Jerry was famous for making promises to potential vendors that time, space, and the physical dimensions of the convention hall could not accommodate.

Ali had been here before, so many times before. It was up to her to figure out how to cool down the heating and cooling blowhard. It was up to her to fix Jerry's mistake.

"Archie, I understand. Here's what I propose." Ali put her hand out to usher him from the center carpet of the main walkway and through several stations currently being constructed for other vendors who had paid extra for the privilege and for the larger spaces. Archie had not. As the purveyor of the third-largest Heating and Cooling company, he'd paid for a standard booth, one outlet, one surge protector, two tables, and table coverings. That was it. And that was all they had. If she gave in, then why would anyone pay the premier booth price? Everyone would know that all you had to do to get a deal was yell at Ali and invoke Jerry.

She needed to smooth this out without making every other vendor feel cheated.

Ali smiled and met Archie's anger with peace and calm.

Archie stood with his arms crossed over his barrel chest. A bull who would not be moved. "This is off the main drag, and I want the main drag." He'd stood where he believed his fiefdom as the owner of the third-largest heating and cooling business in Northwest Ohio entitled him to be.

The venue was arranged as a center main street and then branched out with dozens of grids of smaller walkways. Booths were meticulously spaced and equitably priced. Each booth was assigned and paid for, and some were already set up. She had to stand her ground but make Archie believe he was winning.

"I know you want the center aisle but hear me out. This is the corner like you need. You'll have plenty of space here."

"Yeah, out here in bum f—"

She interrupted before he could utter the rest of his characterization of the location. He felt hidden. He railed that no one would see them here. But here's where Ali's solution kicked in.

"Not at all," Ali told him, "This is right across from Ruby's Hot Dog Stand, see?"

"I'm not selling hotdogs."

"No, but everyone will be here, in line, a captive audience, really. The main drag is great, don't get me wrong, but you'll be the only big vendor with your display in this area. Again, all the space you need." She then lowered her voice to a whisper. She wanted Archie to think she was giving in. "I'll talk to electrical; we'll get your four outlets. Do NOT share that. Plus, you're way smarter in this spot than some." Ali acted as though she was letting him in on a secret.

"Smarter than some?"

Ali looked around, as though a home improvement and building supply trade show spy was hiding somewhere, hoping to gain valuable intel. She lowered her voice further. "True Flame, your chief competitor, is paying premium for the corner booth up front, but this one, Archie, this keeps it at the regular booth price, but with the size you need, and like I said, hot dog eaters."

Archie perked up at the idea of sticking it to True Flame. He walked around and assessed his potential trade show home for the weekend. If he didn't go for this, Ali wasn't sure what else to do. She had already burned most of her morning dealing with this when she was supposed to be checking on the lanyards.

"Okay, this works. I'll call my team to start setting up."

As Archie's mood turned from blustery to partly sunny, Jerry showed up. He'd hidden from Archie and so that Ali would have to deal with it. True to form, and Jerry appeared after she'd managed to fix things. She knew Jerry was lurking and hiding until he knew it was safe. Until she'd made it safe.

Jerry and Archie were two barrel-shaped peas in a pod. Archie was older, his hair crisscrossed in wisps and tufts over his round head. His skin was at least less red now that he had stopped shouting. Archie wore a golf shirt with his company logo. Jerry had a full head of brown hair and was younger by a decade than Archie, but golf shirt, check, pot belly, check.

Jerry fit right in with Archie. Jerry also enjoyed yelling at Ali when something didn't go his way. Delightful. Jerry was all smiles now as he swept over to them.

"Archie! Great to see you!"

The two shook hands. Ali needed to get out of here and get to her next task. Were they done? Was Archie all set?

"Jerry, I was mad, not gonna lie. Thought you were trying to screw me over on this deal, but this will work. We'll make it work for the price."

"What can I say, Ali wrote the wrong thing down on the layout. I told her, 'Get Archie everything and anything he needs for T-Town H&C.' She's pretty, but ya know." Jerry laughed and put his finger to his head to indicate Ali was just pretty. Jerry was the brains and Ali didn't have any. Really nice, Jerry. Ali swallowed and smiled. She'd rather get out of this conversation than prolong it by sticking up for herself.

She thought, at forty-nine, she'd be past this kind of thing. But not where Jerry was concerned.

"I thought that might be the case." Archie and Jerry looked at Ali as though she was a child who'd just spilled her milk at the adult's table.

Jerry had made this mess, assigned Ali to clean it, and now was taking credit for the solution. *Typical.*

Jerry was a "big picture" guy, he liked to say. He got credit for running one of the best venues in Ohio. He got civic awards, he got the salary, he got the golf outings, and he got the long lunches.

Ali did the details; Jerry got the handshakes. *Fine. Whatever.*

She needed to get out of this and on to the next thing, which today, of course, meant swinging by her dad's. He had hospice care now, but she needed to pop in and make sure he was okay. Half of the time that meant sleeping at her dad's. Just in case he needed something.

And "okay" was relative. Her dad didn't have long. And that fact had put a dark cloud over her for the last several months. She was an optimist, a look-forward person, a bright-side oldest daughter. But there was no more bright side to be found with her dad's cancer. They were at the "keep him comfortable" stage.

"Gentleman, I'll get out of your way." She backed out of the conversation and they barely noticed.

No sooner did she leave Archie and Jerry than she was on her phone handling half a dozen other details on her way to the parking garage. Ali walked at a fast pace as she dealt with details from her phone.

The coffee vendor backed out; they'd promised a free cup of coffee to all attendees who arrived before 11 am. She needed to sort that out. She called her food service manager.

"If Black Swamp Beans says no, then I'm going to want you to call Gordon's to get our order for next week's school administrator conference moved to this week. We'll serve the coffee ourselves."

Ali finished that call on her way out of the massive main hall. She unclipped her walkie-talkie and pressed the button. "Carl, you on?"

"Yeah, Boss."

"Don't let Jerry here ya say that," she laughed. Ali wasn't the boss, but her co-workers at Frogtown gave her the respect she didn't get from Jerry.

"Right, like he's on the walkie."

One of the reasons she loved her job was the staff at Frogtown Convention Center. They had become her work family. Jerry got the accolades, but her work family knew the truth about who ran the place. She was glad no one saw her smile at Carl's assessment of Jerry. She never badmouthed Jerry to anyone on staff.

"Stop! Hey, can you make sure they figure out why those lights in the C Corridor are blinking?"

6

"On it. Get out of here, you're going on what? Thirteen hours in this place?"

"Who's counting? I am heading out for a bit."

"How's your dad?"

"Worse, but thanks for asking."

"Consider the lights fixed."

"You're the best!"

Before she entered the parking garage, Ali called her husband. Cell service in the garage was terrible.

Ted Harris, Ph.D., usually didn't answer. He, like Jerry, was too important to handle every call.

She left a message.

"Hey, just checking in. Thought I might grab a bite with you before I head back out?"

She hadn't seen Ted much lately. Between work and her dad, she hadn't paid much attention to her husband. But they'd been married for over twenty years. There were ebbs and flows in their together time as a couple. This was an ebb.

Ali was planning to make it up to Ted with a cocktail party next week to celebrate his tenure.

Oh, dang! That was another call she had to make: confirm with the caterer whether she wanted hot hors d'oeuvres or, the charcuterie board, or both. Well, it was after five. That would have to wait.

She figured her absence of late gave Ted more free time to tool around in his vintage 1989 Porsche 911 Carrera. It was impractical and obscenely expensive, and Ali wasn't allowed near it.

"You'll scratch it," Ted said.

He loved that car, and it was the first thing he got after they were done with their mini-van era. Since the kids had free tuition via Ted's job at the university, he said he'd earned the car.

Ali had her own favorite vehicle. Ali's Dad was a Chrysler retiree, so she'd bought her Grand Cherokee on the friends and family plan at a good discount. She had since paid it off, and she kept it nice. It had four-wheel drive and could haul what she needed. Ted's Porsche was red, and Ali's Jeep was black forest green pearl. She'd keep that Jeep as long as she could. It really was her mobile office.

She got behind the wheel and hit the '80s channel on her radio. A little Bon Jovi to clear the stress of Archie and Jerry out of her mind as she made her way home.

Downtown Toledo was a quick twenty minute drive from just about everywhere else in Toledo, Ohio. The house that she and Ted had restored over the course of their marriage was in a neighborhood called Old Orchard.

She loved her neighborhood of historic homes. The sidewalks were lined with trees, and Ted could even walk to the university if he wanted to. Though he usually drove his flashy car these days.

That was a perk, too. The University of Toledo was a stone's throw away, where both her kids, courtesy of Ted's job and their good grades, were getting college free and clear. Katie and Tye were in their senior and sophomore years in college and despite the poor planning of having two in school at the same time, they were managing the finances better than most. Thanks to that tuition situation.

Ali knew that the big old Tudor-style home might be too big for her and Ted soon, but for now, the kids popped in and out whenever they were on summer break, needed to do laundry, and when they ran out of food in their apartments. Plus, she'd touched every inch of the house during a lifetime of renovations to turn it into this home. DIY and decorating were her therapy.

Ali parked her Jeep in the driveway and made her way into the backdoor. As she walked through the mudroom and into the kitchen, she sighed when she saw what was left there. Dishes in the sink. *Why in the heck didn't Ted ever put them in the stupid dishwasher?*

Alas, that would have to wait. She wanted to change clothes

and grab a bag for tomorrow in case this was the last time she'd be able to pop home with her own busy schedule.

Her big house was creaky. The wood floors crackled and shifted under her shoes as she headed up the stairs to their bedroom.

Ali heard Ted's voice. *Ah, he's on the phone*, she thought.

And then the door to her bedroom opened up.

A lovely young woman, maybe her daughter Katie's age, walked out of Ali and Ted's room. She was wearing one of Ted's polo shirts. The nice one they'd gotten him for Father's Day last year.

"Uh, oh." The girl stopped, clearly startled by Ali's appearance in the hall.

And then a few things shifted into focus that hadn't dawned on her at first.

The woman did not have pants on. Or shoes. And she looked a bit tousled. The evidence mounted up as to what exactly she'd interrupted.

"Star, make sure to order the extra side. I'm hungry."

Ted walked out into the hall, and he had no shirt but, thankfully, did have pants on. Her aging husband looked like Tom Cruise without the HGH. She marveled at how he still looked very much like he did when they met. His jaw was only slightly softer, and his brown hair had a just a tiny sprinkle of white at the temples.

Ali was taking information in, and her brain tried to process it. Maybe she was just as dumb as Jerry indicated. She sure felt dumb right now, incredibly dumb.

"Ali. You said you were going to be gone all night."

"Ha, yes, I did. My apologies." She'd just apologized for interrupting her husband's dalliance in her own house. This would earn her a gold star in the grade book of people pleasing.

"This is awkward," Star said.

"No, it's great. My fault. I'm just going to grab a change of clothes." Ali brushed past Star and Ted. He grabbed her arm.

"If you'd give us a moment, we can discuss—"

Ali whipped around and yanked her arm free. Her brain began to catch up. Her emotions, too, threatened to knock her to her knees or knock Ted's head off his neck.

"I'm busy, Ted. I need to get to my Dad's. If you could strip the bed and put the dirty dishes in the dishwasher? Thanks."

Her words were polite. But her tone was on the edge of murderous. She didn't recognize the sound of her voice.

Ali walked to her closet. She grabbed clothes and underwear, and flung everything into her bag. Somehow, her closet felt alien to her. It was like her brain had shifted in her skull, and everything was different. Altered.

Ted was scrambling to find his shirt, and Star was unfazed, it appeared, by the appearance of the professor's wife.

"If you would have called," Ted said, as though that was the answer to whatever *this* was.

"Ted, I did. Check your voicemail."

She was forming sentences, saying words, and yet it all seemed to be happening in someone else's life. Was she watching this on Netflix? Or was she in the scene? If it were a movie, she'd have thought of something clever to say. She'd be witty. Cutting.

Nothing witty came to mind. Ali wanted out. That's all she could think: *Get out of this house, get out of this scene. Change the channel.*

Ali pushed past Ted and then Star. She ran down the stairs. Two at a time.

Ted wasn't chasing her. That was something. She could extricate herself, and...*What? Think? Call a lawyer? Set the house on fire?* All of these things raced through her head.

Her first bit of clarity arrived as she walked out the kitchen door to the back porch.

She'd parked her Jeep behind the garage because, of course,

10

Ted's vehicle needed the shelter of the small, detached space. "You could hit the side of the garage with your Jeep if you squeeze in there." She remembered his admonition. You're too dumb to use the garage, was the point.

Ted's car sat in that garage. Ding free. It was parked in the center as though it deserved both spaces. Was that a metaphor for their marriage? Ted deserved all the spaces.

She looked around the garage. There was an open bag of topsoil, and it called to her.

She opened the front door of his car and hoisted the bag inside. She ripped open the top of the plastic bag. It was heavy. But she'd fix that.

Ali poured the deep brown dirt all over his leather seats, the stick shift, the dashboard, and the floor mats. She watched it fill in every crevice of his pristine vehicle.

"That's gonna be tough to clean," she said aloud. Ali left the empty bag on the passenger seat.

She surveyed her work. "Well, if Star still doesn't have pants on, she won't have to worry about getting them dirty!" Ali, again, spoke the words aloud. Her voice was still weird but slightly more recognizable.

She was the only one to hear her little quip. Ted and Star were still in her house. Her gorgeous, lovingly restored 1935 Tudor.

It was her home; she'd done everything to make it so for her family. And now, she didn't want to look at it. Ali was more upset that Ted chose to betray her in her own home than if he'd been at some motel. That felt more personal than the cheating. It was like he stole her home at that moment.

Well, she'd stolen the fun of his car, at least until he got it detailed.

Ali brushed the dirt off her hands and got in her Jeep.

She didn't have any more time for this scene. She had to get to her dad's.

ALI

Ali grew up only a few blocks away from the house she'd just fled. That was the great thing about Old Orchard. Everyone from working class to college professors to young families could find a place there. Manor homes and starter cottages sat side-by-side along the tree-lined sidewalks.

Her childhood home was a three-bed, two-bath bungalow. It was small, especially with three girls jockeying for space in the bathroom. Her dad spent most of his time in the detached garage workshop or at the Union Hall. He always thought the house she and Ted bought in the very same neighborhood was too big and too fancy. But he did admire its bones. And back then the bones were the selling point, it needed work, which was reflected in the price and that was how they afforded their stately home. Her home. The home Ted enjoyed with Star. Ugh. Ali thought back to when her dad visited the first time.

"They don't make them like this anymore, I'll give you that," he'd said as he ran his work-calloused palm over the hard plaster walls when he walked through during the inspection.

Over the years, he'd complimented Ali on her restoration skills with the house. It made her happy that he noticed the care she'd taken to restore, not demolish, the place.

She'd updated it and taken care to make things modern without jettisoning the historic character of the home.

Her childhood home was also stuck in time. But her dad didn't worry about modernizing at all. It was a time capsule, really. It was fifteen years since her dad had purchased anything new. Instead, he touched up paint when needed and focused on meticulous maintenance. Style? Well, style wasn't Bruce Kelly's concern.

Bruce Kelly's house was in good repair. It was neatly organized, albeit out of date. The kitchen cabinets were from the 70s. Five years ago, Ali would have just said they were ugly. Now, they sort of seemed groovy when compared to the epidemic of white kitchen cabinets. The plain brown flat front paneled cabinets and harvest gold appliances seemed ironic in today's world. But this place was nothing of the sort. It was their childhood home, décor frozen from the moment their mother died. Bruce kept things in repair and in order, he did not "freshen up the interior design." She remembered being so embarrassed by the kitchen when she compared it to the homes of her more la dee dah friends. They had mauve and teal and everything new. And of course, it all came back around—even 70s kitsch.

Ali put down her bag in the corner of the breakfast nook.

"Darlene? I'm here. Hope I'm not too late."

"Ali, you look tired. You sure you don't want me to call and get a night person to cover?"

"No, just one of those days." Ali didn't feel like describing the two scenes that had surely contributed to her frown lines today.

"Hmm, well, we've talked about you taking the oxygen mask first, you know?"

"I'm fine, really, how's he doing?"

Darlene Effler, the hospice nurse, was an angel on Earth, Ali believed. She was shorter than Ali, so maybe just over five feet tall? But she was all muscle, heart, and practical advice.

They'd called her last month when Dad said no more treatment. Ali wished they'd called her two months sooner for all the compassionate care she'd provided to their whole family.

And as her father lay dying, it was Darlene who made it possible to keep him in his home. It was Darlene who knew how to manage his pain. It was Darlene who could see that Ali had had a doozy of a day.

But even Darlene had limits, and it was time for her to head out and for Ali to clock in for her overnight vigil. They'd been managing things in shifts like this for just under two weeks.

"I think we're down to hours, honey." Darlene's warm hand patted Ali's shoulder.

Ali wanted to cry, accept a hug, and take a shower. But she did none of those things. It felt like letting go of control with a good cry would be akin to a bursting damn. She had her dad to think of, her event at work, her kids, and her little sisters. They all relied on Ali. Ali wasn't going to fall apart. She didn't have time.

"You really think tonight?"

"Maybe."

Darlene was matter-of-fact, and she had answers without histrionics. She understood that Ali didn't want sentiment. She wanted data. She wanted to know so she could prepare. Darlene had been through this dozens of times, but Ali had not. She appreciated the steady guidance and the angel on Earth that was Darlene Effler of Toledo Loving Hospice.

"I'll check in with him and then call my sisters to keep them up to speed."

"Look, you know what to do, right, if he stops breathing, wants medication, anything?"

"You taught me well. Go home."

"Call me if he passes. I'll help you through the next bit."

"Thank you for everything." This time, Ali squeezed Darlene's shoulder. So many families owed her so much, Ali realized. She made the worst situation less so.

Ali put her things in her old room, but likely she'd not sleep there tonight. If Darlene's assessment was accurate, Ali would be sitting bedside, until...well, until whatever.

Bruce Kelly was once a giant of a man, tall, broad, strong, and frightening really. But he was disintegrating now, thanks to cancer. He'd barely said a word for over two weeks.

Ali used to be so afraid of him. He ruled the house as a single dad—a widower who'd had to figure out how to raise three daughters.

He didn't share emotions other than anger, and he didn't walk down memory lane. He told them very little about their mother. What Ali remembered was perfume, pretty hair, and, sometimes, chaos.

Her mother, Joetta Kelly, died in a car wreck when Ali was in second grade. She tried hard to hold onto memories of her mother. But second grade was so very long ago.

Now, it was her father's time. She was about to be a forty-nine-year-old orphan. What would stay with her of Bruce as Ali's life moved forward? Pretty hair and perfume for mommy, gruff strength and motor oil for daddy?

Bruce was not going easy or quickly. But he had been quiet. The stoic nature of Bruce Kelly was intact. His only complaints were having to rely on others these last few months. He was as independent as a man got. But now, even that was washed away.

Ali hoped she was making the decisions he wanted. She committed to caring for him with as much dignity as she could when he couldn't even manage the basics anymore.

"Hi, Dad, I'm here." She brushed her hand gently on his cheek. He stirred. Even that must have hurt.

Ali checked the room. Darlene had it arranged the exact way she would have done it herself. There was a cold pitcher of water and a clean glass with a straw if Bruce needed it. But he hadn't asked for water lately. For days, actually.

That was a sign, she knew.

The room was tidy. The covers on the hospital bed were neatly folded over Ali's father. At one point, he'd been visibly uncomfortable, but now, he lay still in the bed. He breathed in and out but slowly. Darlene had told her to listen for a rattle.

She leaned down to listen to her dad. No rattle.

Ali looked around. There was no laundry in the hamper. Darlene had taken that to the laundry room in the basement. There wasn't even anything to dust.

Ali could sit by the bedside, go to the bedroom down the hall and sleep, or sit in her dad's TV room and watch something.

But she was restless. Reeling. A jumble of images and scenarios played in her mind. What was her priority right now? The implosion of her marriage? The final details of the home and garden show at work? Protecting her nearly adult kids from the knowledge of the implosion of her marriage? Or was it none of the above?

Her father's needs were met, for now. What was the productive and useful thing to do after what she'd been through today?

Ali found herself wandering around the house. She and Faye, her middle sister, had convinced Dad to get rid of the shag carpet and the orange countertops, small updates. But not enough. She wondered what a future buyer would think of this place—Bruce Kelly's well-maintained time capsule.

It was a three-bedroom ranch house south of Kenwood, on Densmore. Ali lived on a double lot at Barrington and Christie. Her dad's place didn't have the grandeur of some of the homes near her. It was perfect, though, for her working-class dad, her union-strong dad.

They didn't make them like her dad anymore, she knew. That was good and bad, she also knew.

He'd raised three little girls with no feminine side of his own to tap into. He barely tolerated their Caboodles of Bonnie Bell and clouds of White Rain. She'd spent her life tiptoeing around his temper.

This house had all those memories. She looked at the framed pictures on the china hutch that sat in the dining room. Senior pictures of Faye, Blair, and her. A picture of her Grandma and Grandpa Kelly, and of course, Bruce with his beloved Starcraft fishing boat.

He'd given the boat up a few years ago. He'd loved putting it in at Devil's Lake in the Irish Hills. Alas, he never pulled the trigger to buy a cottage there. Too bad, that would have been a nice family memory. Too late though, property in the Irish Hills was too expensive these days.

He worked. That's what Bruce Kelly did. He worked. He paid for this house and fine-tuned it to proper working order. Over and over.

And now what? Would she move back in here so Professor Can't Keep It In His Pants could live happily ever after with— what's her name? Oh, yeah, Star.

She wandered around the house three times and realized she needed her sisters. Darlene had said her dad did, too, and that this could be it.

There was no way Blair could get there tonight, but Faye could. Ali would worry about how to handle the disaster that was her marriage after she'd handled whatever came next with Bruce Kelly.

She texted Faye.

Hey, Dad's okay right now, but we're on death rattle watch. Darlene's assessment.

Got it, packing a bag. One hour?

I think.

Faye lived in Sylvania, close by, but not as close as Ali did.

An hour.

Ali continued wandering around, until suddenly, from down

17

the hall, she heard her father's voice. Ali rushed back to his bedside. He was mumbling. His head moved from side to side. She also heard the rattle. The end was close, as Darlene predicted.

"Hey, Dad."

She got the water and put the straw to his lips. He lifted his head and sipped a drop.

"I did it to keep you three safe."

"What?" *Is this a hallucination? What was he talking about?*

"You understand? I am sorry, but it was bad. You could have died."

"I could have died?"

She had no idea what he was talking about.

"I need you to know! I'm sorry. It was the only way."

"Nothing to be sorry about."

"I tried to do the best. But I'm not her. I couldn't be her."

"Mom? Are you talking about Mom?"

He never talked about their mom. The memories Ali had were fleeting, precious, and never enhanced with the help of her father. *Was he talking about Mom now? Did he see her?*

"Okay, Dad, it's okay."

He'd never expressed anything but gruff confidence in his life as their father. Never a moment of parenting doubt. Was this the last thing he'd think about? A final worry?

"It had to be done. Cut off. The only way," he continued haltingly. "I thought—I'm sorry—Tell Faye and Blair."

As he said it, Faye walked in.

"Dad, I'm here too." She sat down on the other side of the bed and gave Ali a look. Ali answered with a look of her own. A look that let Faye know she had no more idea of her father's intentions than Faye, who'd just walked in.

"Blair, my Blair."

"Sure, Dad, it's Blair." Her father kept mistaking Faye for Blair. Blair lived in Cincinnati. She'd come in and out when she could work remotely. Blair had done her best to sit bedside and help relieve her two older sisters. But Blair was not there at this last moment.

She'd never make it in time. Cincinnati was four hours away. The rattle Darlene warned about did not last that long.

Faye didn't seem upset that in her father's mind, The Middle Daughter was unremarkable. He'd switched Faye for Blair. He'd called her "My Blair." Blair was Bruce Kelly's favorite. They all knew that and didn't hold it against her. Blair was easy to love the most.

Ali didn't want to accept it, though. She was there to fight for both her sisters, whether they were the middle or littlest.

"Dad, it's Faye and Ali."

"Yes, Faye. Sweet Faye. I'm sorry about that, too. What a lucky man I was. I had the best three daughters."

Ali blinked back tears. An awkward squeeze of the hand when she'd walked down the aisle was the closest Bruce Kelly got to effusive affection. This was the sweetest thing he'd ever said to them.

And it was also the last thing he said. Bruce Kelly, father of three, Jeep retiree, Vietnam veteran, settled back in his bed.

He closed his eyes.

The rattle got raspier.

Just before dawn, even the rattle stopped.

Three

DIDI

Didi Rivera stared at the pool. Green. It was green. *How did it get this bad?*

Jorge always took care of it. He loved taking care of it. But right now, that was impossible. She needed to hire a pool guy, just temporarily, until Jorge was better.

Didi didn't have extra hands to fish around in the pockets of her shorts for her phone. *Oh, good grief.* Where had she left it? She was always leaving it somewhere. She swished the skimmer over the green water. This wasn't helping.

Her grandkids had phones permanently attached to their physical person. She was usually annoyed by it, but maybe it was an advantage. She was always being told to keep her phone "on" for everything from getting around town to when Jorge's pills were ready at the pharmacy. If she had the thing attached to her physical person like those grandkids, maybe she wouldn't always be looking for the darn thing.

Finding the phone needed to take a backseat. She needed to

argue with her husband at this particular moment. Jorge was slowly approaching, very slowly, but sternly lecturing her.

"What are you doing out here, Didi? I said I'd get to it." He tried to take the skimmer pole away from her.

"I'm just getting leaves out. Keep your hands to yourself, or we'll both wind up in the bog that ate our swimming pool."

He stopped trying to stop her. And it was clear he probably needed to take a minute to catch his breath.

Jorge's salt and pepper hair was mostly salt now. His brown skin was tan, as always. He was still the most handsome man she'd ever seen. But that wasn't why she loved him. Well, it wasn't the only reason. Among other things, he was honest, sappy, corny, loved to dance with her, and was quite literally the hardest-working man she'd ever met.

And that was the problem. He was supposed to be resting.

They'd kept the Sea Turtle Resort running smoothly for almost fifteen years now. It was their "retirement plan." However, they'd never stopped working. She knew sitting around and trying to relax would kill Jorge just as fast as it would bore her to death, too.

She'd been officially retired from her job and going stir crazy when a private equity firm offered Jorge an early retirement package from his job. He had been the maintenance manager for the sprawling Island Winds Resorts in St. Pete. They had both decided to take this place on. She managed the bookings and the activities; he managed the grounds of the Sea Turtle's hotel and beach cottages. It was a tiny operation compared to the Island Winds, so they handled it easily. Well, they used to.

For the first time in their lives, even though they were in their 70s, she thought they might actually need to retire.

Complications from Jorge's hip replacement were making this season the toughest yet. His hip wasn't ready for the off-season work they needed to do. And try as she might, Didi didn't know how to replace the vacuum hose for this pool. Nor could she haul the chlorine from the truck to the pool shed. Skimming the surface of this pool wasn't going to fix the bigger issue.

All of it was getting to Jorge, who'd been meticulous about the grounds at the Sea Turtle.

"Jorge! You're supposed to call me when you walk around."

"Didi! You're supposed to have your phone on you. At all times. I called you, and it went straight to voicemail." She had no argument for that.

She knew the Sea Turtle Resort had seen better days, just like her and Jorge.

The six cottages and adjacent motel were looking...well, she hated to say it, shabby. She knew it, and Jorge knew it.

Didi Rivera was not ready to quit, though, not yet.

But she had to figure something out. They couldn't go on forever as managers of this place. She loved it so, though.

"Sit down. You're going to have to talk me through how to shut this pump off until we can get it fixed." The pool's mechanical elements were making funny noises.

"I can fix it."

"No, not right now you can't." She raised her voice. She rarely did that, but she wanted Jorge around. They had married in their forties and had been together for over thirty years, but she wanted more time. Sure, they were both in their seventies, but other than that hip of his and her stupid phone being missing all the time, they were good. They had many good years left, God willing.

What they didn't have was the strength or energy for all that needed managing here. The quirky little resort may as well be the Island Winds. It felt impossible without a fully functioning Jorge!

"Fine. Fine. I'll talk you through it, and we'll call Silvio from the pool place. He can do this until I am back to full strength."

"Silvio, I was trying to find his number and then realized I couldn't find my phone. Ugh. Okay, but sit." She put a hand out to the lounge chair and helped him ease into it.

Before she had Jorge completely settled into this spot, Karen

Ort, the current occupant of the Key Lime Cottage, walked briskly onto the pool deck and got right in Didi's face.

"I want a full refund."

"Excuse me?"

"The listing showed a beautiful blue pool. This is a green mess. The listing showed the courtyard filled with tropical foliage. There's a frigging lake-sized puddle of water in the center of an overgrown jungle that is breeding mosquitos with goodness knows what kind of diseases. My little Claxton was bit so bad he's got a welt the size of a baseball on his arm. Full refund. Full."

"We apologize for the pool; we are in the midst of contacting our—"

"—It's too late; we have seven days of vacation, and it's ruined. Completely and utterly ruined."

Didi winced. She felt each word like a knife in her chest. They'd prided themselves on running this little gem. The Sea Turtle Resort had been hosting visitors to Haven Beach, Florida, since 1948. It was a resort before Haven Beach was even a town!

She knew they had let a lot of things slip. But she took it seriously, the accusation that they'd ruined anyone's vacation. Or their impression of Haven Beach.

"I know the pool is out of commission, but Mrs. Ort, the beach, the sand, I am sure Claxton would enjoy that even more."

The Sea Turtle Resort was directly on Haven Beach. The Gulf of Mexico provided a spectacular sunset show every night. How could anyone see that as ruined?

"Really? Well, since we don't have clean beach towels or a working air conditioner, I'd say a day at the beach isn't quite enough to make up for it."

Didi nodded. It wasn't what was promised. She knew it. All she could do now to please this guest was to refund her money.

"I'll put it all back on the credit card we have on file."

"As you should. And we need help with the bags." Karen turned and walked away.

Jorge would normally help with the bags. He tried to get out of the lounge chair. Didi saw him grip the handles to gather the strength to withstand the pain of it.

"NO! You sit. I'll get the roller cart and get Karen out of here. We'll regroup after she's gone."

"Honey, you need to be careful, too, your blood pressure."

"My blood pressure, your hip, this green pool. We're in a little bit of a pickle. But you know what? We've got the best view in Florida, and that's what I call a blessing."

She bent over the lounge chair and kissed Jorge.

"Well, I'm not sure it's the best view. Second best."

"What?" She was appalled; they *did* have the best view, the best beach here!

"I've got the best view watching you walk away." He raised an eyebrow to let her know he was referring to her seventy-five-year-old backside.

"Jorge, you're terrible." Didi's face got warm. Still, after all these years, he could make her blush.

She turned around and felt a swat on that same backside as she went off to find the luggage cart they kept in the laundry building.

She could hear Karen barking orders to Claxton and her entire family. *What an unpleasant woman.*

Didi tried not to smile too broadly. If Karen et al. didn't see what a gem Haven Beach was, that was her problem. Didi knew. And so did Jorge.

Four

FAYE

Faye looked at her sister, Ali. *How was she so unruffled?* In the middle of a hurricane, Faye's big sister Ali was a rock. Always.

"Thank you for coming." Ali smiled and accepted hug after hug. The American Legion Hall was packed with mourners.

Ali was the big sister in all things, a substitute mother in a lot of ways, even though they were only two years apart.

Ali seemed to have everything under control in all scenarios.

And she was still so beautiful at forty-nine.

Her big sister was the captain of the cheerleaders and the president of the Honor Society. She had thick ash-blonde hair that, these days, she always had in a ponytail or clipped up out of the way. Ali used to have the most gorgeous highlights in the summer.

Faye was worried about Ali, though.

In the dead of winter, in Toledo, at this funeral, it looked very much like Ali needed Vitamin D or a nap or better concealer. Then again, they were in the thick of it right now.

Caring for and then burying Bruce Kelly had sucked. Faye was numb, too. And she'd done half as much as Ali.

Ali Kelly Harris was a superstar in Faye's eyes. But even through the lens of love, she saw the truth. Ali's eyes were tired. Two dark circles under them looked almost like bruises.

In the last seven days, Ali had confidently made calls, sympathetically informed distant cousins of the news, decided on a casket, taken in a million casseroles, and managed to make a potluck at the Conn Weissenberger American Legion Hall look like a catered affair.

Bruce Kelly wasn't all that religious, but he was very patriotic. He was the proud son of a World War II vet and served with the Marine Corps in Vietnam.

It made sense, holding this gathering at the hall, with its dropped ceiling, wood chair rale, and rows and rows of white table-cloth covered eight tops filling the space. There was a bar on the far end of the room where they'd set up coffee, soda pop, and water for mourners. The large kitchen featured a serving window. American flags, lists of members, founders, and trophies were randomly displayed. And there was plenty of parking. Ali also pointed out that all of Dad's old cronies would be able to find it. There was nothing fancy or pretentious, but it was serviceable and familiar. Plus, the Kelly Sisters knew exactly how to run an event here.

They'd had Ali's wedding reception here. Nothing fancy for the Kelly Sisters. Somehow, the sisters made every gathering sparkle. They were sort of known for it.

But really it was Ali. She was the engine behind any magical moment that Faye and Blair had ever experienced.

Faye thought back to this space, this hall. Dad said graduation parties were "ridiculous."

"You're not accomplishing a darn thing getting out of high school. I expect it. Welcome to work!" That's what he told Ali.

Dad hadn't let Ali have a grad party. Even though Faye knew

everyone at Whitmer High School would have attended a party for her big sister. Ali was friends with everyone! But no, no party. Bruce Kelly put his foot down on that one. Faye remembered her father putting his foot down a lot.

When Faye graduated two years later, Ali had taken charge. She hadn't listened to Bruce Kelly's rule about what should be celebrated. Ali had insisted. She'd rented this hall, enlisted her friends to cook food, and strung Christmas lights all over the ceiling. The place had looked amazing! Faye Kelly had the grad party of Ali's dreams.

Of course, by the time Blair graduated, Bruce had revised his thinking and allowed them to rent a shelter house at Olander Park, all the way out in Sylvania. It was practically fancy by Kelly standards. Even then you could see Ali's career path developing. She was so good at planning the best parties. And now, she was doing it for the entire town at the Frogtown Convention Center. And, of course, not getting the credit she deserved. Ugh. It drove Faye up the wall. Ali was why that place was always booked and everyone had good experiences in downtown Toledo.

Faye turned her attention to her younger sister, Blair.

Ali had made that call, too. Faye could still hear it, see it. Ali telling Blair, with a gentle tone, that Dad had passed. "I know, sweetie. He loved you so much. It's okay."

Ali had comforted Blair. But who comforted Ali? Faye tried, but it was easy to see the coping mechanism Ali had employed their entire lives was action oriented. Do things. Keep busy!

Blair Kelly lived in Cincinnati. Four hours away by car. Her job in IT could be done remotely, so that was good. But it was also bad. She could never fully leave the office.

Faye had seen Blair step out and log on to her work laptop several times in the last three days. You'd think someone else could cover her job during her father's funeral?

Ali made sure Blair didn't have any responsibilities other than just being here. She'd told Blair as much when she'd made that initial phone call.

"There's nothing to be done right now. We're going to have services on Thursday. Just get here by then."

Ali was making it easier for Blair. Faye tried to make it easier for Ali. Yet Ali hadn't cracked, not once, since all this started.

Dad had died at 2 am on a Tuesday, and by noon that day, Ali had most of the details arranged. Visitation and services were set for Thursday.

As they accepted hugs and well wishes from Bruce's crew at the plant, fellow Jeep retirees, and a few of the Kelly cousins from Flat Rock in Michigan, Faye realized she'd not helped her sister at all. She'd just done as Ali asked. Maybe that was a help?

Faye walked over to Ali and stood beside her. Ali was accepting another hug graciously. This hug was from Ollie Hoolihan, an old friend and fellow Jeep retiree. He had ideas and he was letting Ali know all about them.

"We need to name the Euchre tournament after him. That's what I'm working on. He started it, you know, back in 1977. We even did it in the Blizzard of '78!"

"Ah, that's lovely, Ollie, he did love Euchre."

Bruce Kelly had taught his three girls how to drive a stick shift, change their own tires, and "go it alone" in Euchre. That memory of their dad almost made Faye cry. She blinked away the tears threatening to form.

Ollie squeezed Faye into a hug. She'd worked at the plant with him for a brief stint before he retired. He squeezed her hard, the breath coming out of her lungs a little.

These old guys, there weren't many of them left. She was actually a veteran now at Jeep. She was closer to retiree than newbie. Her thirty and out was around the corner. How had that happened? How had life moved this fast? She supposed her dad thought the same. His deathbed ramblings indicated regret and remorse, but also love. Deep love from the man who put his foot down.

Why hadn't he said any of those things before? Ugh. Faye didn't want to get pulled into a spiral of grief, of mid-life what-ifs. It felt so cliché.

Old Ollie turned away from the sisters and ambled toward the door. The crowd was thinning now.

Faye put an arm around Ali.

Blair appeared on the other side of their big sister.

"The Bruce Kelly Euchre Tournament? Dad would hate that," Faye said.

"It seems kind of sweet," Blair replied. Their little sister was the tallest of them and the most wide-eyed about what Dad would like or not like. The short answer was he would not like almost everything.

"But dad didn't like to draw attention, on him, on us, you know the way he was," Faye said, then added in her best Bruce Kelly working man gruff voice, "Quit showing off."

"You fishin' for compliments?" Ali chimed in with her own impression.

"Oh, alright, alright. I get it," Blair said.

"What can we do to finish up?" Faye asked Ali.

"I'm going to load the flowers and take them to the nursing home, and then I need to head to the Frogtown offices. We've got that home show starting tomorrow, and I've got loose ends there."

"They can't possibly expect you to be there!" Blair protested.

"They don't, but they do. My boss is fairly useless on the details."

"Your dad just died. They shouldn't expect you to be there," Faye backed Blair up.

"It's a good distraction. And you're checking in on your computer for your work, same thing," Ali said.

"Look," Faye replied. "We'll do the flowers. You go to your

office, and then we'll meet up at Dad's. I'm going to pick up a couple of pies from JoJo's Pizza, and we'll just decompress."

"What about the kids?"

"Your two are taking mine to their place."

Faye's son Sawyer was a Freshman at Ohio State University. He could stay at home with Faye while he was here, but it was probably way more fun to hang out at Katie and Tye's. Heck, Faye would like to do that, too. Just have a six-pack and be glad you're not old! Woo hoo! But JoJo's Pizza was damn good, so the Kelly Sisters' post-funeral slumber party was a decent option after the week they'd had—heck, the last six months they'd had since Dad's diagnosis.

"You're both doing okay?" Ali asked with concern. She was worried about her sisters, their kids, the guests, and her job. Faye wondered how long Ali could really keep this all up.

Ali still looked so much like the one picture they had of their mom, blonde and blue-eyed. That is, if she'd had the good fortune to age. Their mom hadn't lived to get wrinkled. So many dark thoughts were popping into Faye's head. It was maddening.

Faye had pinned her own chestnut hair into a bun. It was the color of Dad's, a fact she used to hate, but now, not as much. Now that she was a supervisor and not on the line, she had let it grow a little. Their Blair had almost red hair. Dad said redheads were his favorite. Of course.

Faye wanted to let Ali know they could help. That they could lighten the load. "We both have it covered. See you at Dad's unless you have to get back to Ted."

Ali stiffened.

Faye noticed her reaction. Ted had been dutifully there, greeted guests, and made small talk, but come to think of it, the closest she'd seen Ted to Ali was with Katie and Tye between them.

"What's up, big sister?" Faye asked.

"Yeah, no, on that back to Ted thing. In fact, I've got to call a lawyer. Do you think I can get a discount, a twofer of will reading and divorce filing?"

"What?" Blair and Faye asked in unison. Talking in unison was a common occurrence among the Kelly Sisters.

"Yeah, the day Dad died, I caught Ted with a grad assistant in my house." Ali's jaw was clenched. A deep frown line had set in between her blue eyes.

"I'm going to kick him in the—"

"Faye, that's ridiculous. I already hit him where it hurts the most," Ali interrupted.

"His car?" Blair guessed.

"Ha, yeah, dumped a bag of potting soil all over it. Well, in it."

That was so unlike Ali! Faye was proud. *Take that; you rat bastard cheater!*

The sisters encircled Ali. She accepted the hugs briefly but then brushed them off.

"I don't have time to break down, you know? If you hug me I might—" She stopped and put the back of her hand to her mouth.

She was holding in so much, Faye knew. It couldn't be healthy. *When would Ali get a chance to grieve? Or even a day off?*

"Look, we'll do the flowers. You go deal with your boss. I will try not to assault Ted in the meantime and then take out JoJo's Pizza at Dad's."

"I can't promise that *I* won't assault Ted," Blair added.

Ali gave a little chuckle.

That was good, at least, a little laugh.

"Okay, okay, see you tonight."

Five

ALI

Ted was smart enough to stay out of Ali's way. That was the best he could muster in terms of love and affection. It had dawned on her in the last few days how much she didn't need this man in a practical sense. The man she'd spent her entire adult life with would only slow her down right now. She had things to do. The business of closing out a man's life was full-time work, and Ali already had a job.

They didn't really have any additional words or a fight about the cheating.

Ted had called in a rage about the car, but then she'd trumped his dirty car with her dying dad.

"My Dad has hours, Ted. Call a car detailer and send Star the bill."

Ted had made respectful appearances at her dad's funeral services. He'd made himself scarce when she packed a bag so she could live at her dad's place for a few more days. It just made sense.

She did not want to be near Ted, and she had a lot to do to pack up the old house for sale.

Eventually, they'd need to talk. Ali knew this. But she didn't have the emotional bandwidth for it.

She'd managed the funeral, spent a little time with her sweet sisters, but then rolled right into the home show. She knew Jerry couldn't manage it without her, so she was there.

By Sunday afternoon, after a week of nonstop competency in the face of disasters, Ali was cooked. Death, divorce, and home show mini disasters had frazzled her usually very patient nerves. She hadn't gotten more than four hours of sleep a night for a week.

The last of the home show booths were finally being packed up when Jerry and the Chief of Staff to the Mayor of Toledo, strolled through.

"Huge success, huge!" boomed Jerry.

The Mayor's Chief of Staff, Dale Zarecki, had ushered the mayor in and out for handshakes on the final day. Zarecki wore a Strong for Toledo t-shirt with the mayor's name on the back. Election season was never over, she knew. This event was successful, so somehow, the mayor's office was going to add that to their list of accomplishments. Even though Frogtown was privately owned, politicians liked to call Frogtown their crown jewel. *Whatever.*

Ali didn't have time to shmooze. She couldn't remember when she'd last sat down to eat a meal since the pizza with her sisters. She needed to get out of here sooner rather than later. Let Jerry deal with the bigwigs.

"I hear Ali here signed a record number of builders," Dale said. "Impressive!"

"Oh, Ali, ha, well, she is a great assistant and executes my vision," Jerry said to Dale.

Dale nodded, and what had been a nice compliment from Dale to her turned into Jerry grabbing sole credit.

"On that, Ali, can you get Dale and the mayor's office the swag bags? They all need t-shirts and the goodies!"

The office where they had locked up all the remaining swag bags was across the conference space and two floors up. It was a twenty-minute trip. She also wasn't about to ask any other staff to do it. They were all tired and working OT to button up the conference space.

Ali was currently managing logistics for four trucks vying to use the two spaces available in the loading dock. Vendors who needed the trucks were lining up, demanding their turn. She had a text, a phone call, and a walkie-talkie conversation going at the same time. She pressed the talk button on her walkie.

"Tell Pam's Patio Pavers to wait fifteen minutes; if they go first, it will hold up the rest of the row."

"Ali, did you hear me?" Jerry raised his voice.

"I did. Yes, I'll get Carrie to send over the swag bags Monday morning." Ali smiled at Jerry and Dale, and Dale shifted on his feet.

Jerry stepped forward and got in Ali's face. "I said, go get the bags yourself, *now*, this is the mayor's office. We don't make them wait."

He was yelling. Straight up yelling at her.

The walkie talkie lit up. "Ali, Pam's Patio won't wait. They're moving in front of T.T.'s Inground Pools."

"This is your priority." Jerry poked Ali on the shoulder. He was clearly trying to look like the big man in front of Dale.

Ali's phone was now buzzing. Another issue. Another fire to put out. She ignored the finger poke to the shoulder and glanced at her phone.

"Ali!" Jerry poked again, his voice louder this time.

Zero respect. Zero appreciation.

"I'm ordering you to help Dale immediately. This is your priority."

Jerry had no idea what needed to be prioritized to break down the convention space and be sure each vendor left happy, so they signed up next year at a higher rate. Breaking down was just as important as setting up.

"Ali!"

Jerry was doing this now? He was *really* doing this? Ali snapped. It was the poke on the shoulder that broke the camel's back.

"Jerry. Get them yourself. I quit."

"What?"

"Yep, I quit. Get the swag, deal with Pam's Patio—oh, also the plumbing staff needs to be alerted. Clogged stalls in the second cor —wait. No. Here."

Ali handed the walkie to Jerry. He'd never once asked her about her dad. He'd expected her complete availability. He'd taken credit yet again for all she'd done here. And now? Now he was yelling at her in front of important people to make himself look important.

"You walk out of here now; you'll never work in Toledo again!"

Ali put her hand in the air and waved him off like a gnat.

"I'm calling security. Turn in your badge!" His voice echoed in the cavernous space.

"Yeah? What extension are they? And I'm QUITTING Jerry, you're not firing me."

She left Jerry to have his meltdown while she had hers.

Her office. She needed to get to her office. She took the stairs two at a time instead of the elevator. The fatigue she'd felt was now burned away by anger, adrenaline, and relief. She unlocked her office and stepped inside. She closed the door behind her. She didn't want to talk to Jerry. She didn't want anyone to say, "Be reasonable." She was operating on pure emotion, instinct, and maybe self-preservation, though it probably looked like self-destruction.

Ali looked around. She wasn't one to personalize her office space. This was command central. Not her home. She had one framed photo of her kids at her side at Tye's graduation. She put that in her bag.

Every contact, calendar, memo was in her phone. There was no Rolodex to worry about. She had anyone she'd ever needed to know in her pocket. Her lifetime of efficiency meant this office was easy to clean out.

Ali eyed her Toledo Walleye Mug. She did like that. It went in her big messenger bag. She scanned the space again. Oh yeah, her Toledo Mud Hens ball cap. She always kept it on the hook in the middle of her door. It came in handy when her hair wasn't cooperating after working all night here. She wore it when Toledo's Favorite Son, Jamie Farr, was the headliner of the *M*A*S*H* Fan Convention Frogtown hosted a few years ago.

She put the navy-blue ball cap on her head. Okay, yeah, that was it. That was all she needed.

Ali walked out of Frogtown feeling lighter than she'd felt in months.

But with no idea of what would come next.

Six

ALI

Up until one week ago, if something like this had happened, Ali would have talked to Ted about it.

But Ali didn't call Ted. She didn't call her sisters. She'd quit her job without anyone's two cents about it.

She did talk to her former co-workers though.

Some came to her dad's house with their pleas for her to stay. In between packing her dad's stuff, she listened to them vent.

"Don't leave us!"

"I'm calling the board; you shouldn't be his assistant. It should be the other way around."

"If 13ABC or 11 News knew how much you did to make Frogtown a success, you'd be the woman of the year."

She had done that. And she was proud of it. But Ali felt done. No amount of sweet talk from co-workers could change her mind.

And the truth is, no one is indispensable. They'd find a new manager.

She'd miss them, and they were a good team. A team she'd

built. And one she'd loved leading. Ali had gone to bat for them with Jerry when they deserved raises. She'd put out fire after fire and knew how to handle whatever crisis occurred at Frogtown Convention Center.

And there was always another crisis. She didn't mind that. She liked solving each problem. She loved managing the vendors, the staff, and the visitors. She just didn't love doing it for Jerry.

Ali knew what Ted would say. He had said it many times when she was frustrated about work. Ted would have told her to suck it up. Play nice. He'd have told her to get along. All the while, she'd listen to his tirades about being passed over for tenure or a colleague getting a paper published that he'd deemed "sophomoric."

Well, he had tenure now and a grad assistant girlfriend to accessorize his rise. She didn't want Ted's career counseling any more than she wanted to work with Jerry another day.

Ali was at a crossroads in every phase of her life. She'd quit her job, her husband had quit their marriage, their kids were happily in college, and her aging father was done aging.

All she could think to do was busy herself organizing her childhood home.

She boxed up Bruce Kelly's clothes, looked through old albums, and slept. She needed sleep more than anything else.

Over the next few days, one question emerged.

Who was she now?

Who did she want to be?

More than once, she wondered, if her mother was here, what would she say.

Her mother was denied the luxury of a mid-life crisis. *Was that what this was? Midlife?*

* * *

Two weeks after Bruce Kelly died, the Kelly Sisters officially learned what they already knew. His house and assets were to be split among his three daughters.

Blair wasn't in attendance for the formality, but there wasn't much to decide. The lawyer explained the process. Knowing they would get the house, Ali had already polled her sisters. No one wanted to live in the old Kelly house. Their lives had all moved on from their childhood in the house on Densmore.

Ali had called a real estate agent the day after Bruce passed. Lingering or waiting was bad business in this market. Demand was hot in this neighborhood, and the house was meticulously cared for.

As was their family dynamic. Ali handled it all, including the fielding of offers for Dad's house.

"I've got three offers on the table. Two cash and one financed, but the financed offer sweetened the deal by adding ten grand over asking."

"Oh, yeah, go with that one," Blair said.

"I agree," Faye chimed in as well.

Three to zip. Sell to the highest bidder.

There was no hurry, but there was also no hold-up. Bruce Kelly, the working man, had paid his mortgage years ago. He'd lived frugally. He'd saved.

He'd died with three hundred thousand dollars after all was liquidated to split among his three girls.

"We're heiresses!" Faye joked.

"Sure, yeah, well, we need to be smart. You need to be smart." Ali pointed to Blair, who tended to buy the first thing that struck her fancy. As evidenced by the mirror workout thing she'd bought that was in her Cinci apartment collecting dust.

"Oh, come on, just one dumb thing."

Cinci could be expensive. At least this money would put Ali's mind at ease about her baby sister. She'd be able to pay rent for a few months! Maybe even a whole year. But while it was great, a windfall for sure, it wasn't quit your job money. Which, of course, she'd done, regardless of Bruce Kelly's last will and testament.

Faye threatened to buy a Harley, but in truth, she was just as frugal as Dad. Her weakness was plants. She'd buy every annual at the Toledo Flower Market Sale and then some.

What was Ali's weakness? Not having a dream? Not having any idea how to splurge? She'd been so careful. All this time. She hadn't cultivated the muscle required to kick up her heels.

But thanks to Dad, she did have some time—not a lot of time, but some. She didn't have to replace her income from Frogtown immediately.

But she would have to find a place to live. Soon.

In the meantime, she had two weeks to clear out fifty years at Densmore. So that was her focus. Cleaning out the old family home.

She could do that. She was organized, methodical, and knew every contractor in Toledo. She knew exactly how to move, ship, dispose of, and repair stuff if needed.

Instead of overthinking her career, her marriage, and her midlife malaise, she handled things at the house.

One room at a time.

Bruce Kelly was neat and tidy and non-sentimental, which made going room by room mostly painless.

The death of their father had Ali thinking about their mother, Joetta Kelly. She was young, so very young, when she became a mother, and too young to die.

Bruce hadn't let his girls indulge in maudlin emotions. That they were motherless wasn't his fault. He expected them to all get on with it.

But now, as she worked through the grief of his death, she couldn't quite get on with her mother's death even though it had been a lifetime.

Ali was nine years old when she was drafted into service as the person who took care of food, pigtails, and Christmas gifts for the

Kelly Sisters. Faye was seven and said she remembered their mom in bits. Blair was a toddler when it happened, so the memories weren't really memories. They were stories that Faye and Ali told Blair about having a mom.

Were they together now, Bruce and Joetta? She didn't know if that sounded like a happy ending or not. What she remembered of her mother and father together was fraught. They argued, they screamed.

Well, maybe they had that happily ever after somewhere, if not here.

Remembering the brief time she shared this Earth with both parents was connected to shouting from Bruce and tears from her pretty little mother.

As Ali pressed on and packed the house, she didn't find one article of clothing or memento of her mother. Her father had excised it all after the car accident that claimed their mother.

Once, when she asked to visit their mother's burial site, Bruce explained she'd been cremated, and the ashes were at the lake. He'd taken his wife to the lake once or twice, and she'd liked it. "She liked being on a beach." He had said, offering a tiny morsel of memory to a daughter starving for more details.

By the time Ali made her way to cleaning out Bruce's workshop in the garage, the house was pretty well buttoned up. The garage workshop was the last of the things to sort through.

Tools, cans of nails, bits of wood from the projects he'd done around the house, and a tin case of drill bits of every size were all that remained. Should they sell all this or maybe just donate it to Habitat for Humanity? Ali had worked with Habitat over the years. She decided to give them a call to see if they wanted the snow blower, or the circular saw, or the set of wrenches.

She looked around the workshop, built into the narrow length of the garage, and remembered there was an attic up there.

"Ugh, I forgot about that." She said aloud to herself.

There was a little rope trailing down, so she tugged at it. The attic stairs unfurled. This was where they'd kept old Christmas lights and boxes of magazines Bruce had gotten from their grandpa. He said Grandpa insisted the magazines were "collector's items," but Bruce called them junk. Bruce didn't like junk cluttering up his space. Ali was glad of it now. She'd heard horror stories of Hummels and baseball cards and egg cartons to be disposed of after her friends' parents passed. This was a gift Bruce gave to her, no clutter.

Ali climbed the ladder. She was going to have to dress in more layers if the attic was packed with stuff. It was freezing in the garage. Toledo in January was no joke, weather-wise.

She pulled a cord in the center of the attic space, and a single lightbulb flickered on.

There were cardboard boxes on top of boxes, but they were all stacked neatly. This was a relief; she could manage these. She could bring them down one at a time.

She scanned the writing on the outside of each box.

Taxes. Halloween Costumes. Bulbs.

Yep, no surprises there.

Each box was clearly marked.

She'd deal with it tomorrow. It would likely take a morning to bring these down, and it would also likely take a dose of Advil to recover from the task.

She positioned herself at the ladder to go back down and then one box caught her eye.

It had no label.

Hmm.

She crouched over to it and on the top, very small, were the letters *JB*.

The box was taped shut with masking tape that had gone brittle with age.

Her mother's initials. Joetta Bowles.

Was this it? Was this the only thing left of Bruce Kelly's marriage?

And if it was their mother's stuff, why hadn't he ever let them see it?

Ali was irritated anew by Bruce Kelly's stern streak.

She decided to grab the box and bring it down. She'd look through this one box tonight and tackle the rest tomorrow.

It was no easy task, navigating the ladder-like stairs with the big box in one arm and her hand on the ladder itself.

"If I break a hip doing this..." Ali muttered to herself as she made her way down. She managed to set her two feet back on the solid concrete floor of the garage without loss of life and limb.

She was getting cold, though. She wanted to open this box immediately but also wanted to warm up.

"Okay, JB, let's get inside, get some coffee, and see what's what."

She'd tackle this box when the feeling returned to her fingers and toes.

A short while later, as coffee brewed from her dad's ancient ("It works just fine!") Mr. Coffee machine, Ali stood at the kitchen table.

She had the kitchen shears at the ready, but they weren't necessary. The tape peeled off easily, and the old cardboard came with it in some sections.

"Geez, Dad, has this been sealed since Mom died?"

She thought back to what her dad looked like back then, really for most of his life. He was strong. At six feet, he was tall for an Irishman, her grandma used to say. He was military in his bearing, meticulous in his grooming, but utilitarian. He was a man who went to the barber, shaved every day, and kept everything ship shape but nothing "froofy," as he called anything that had the whiff of feminine energy—no cologne or hair products for Bruce Kelly.

She needed to do that more often, force her mind's eye to put the younger Bruce in place of the one she'd just watched die.

It wasn't fair to the pillar of strength that he was to hang on to what he looked like in the end.

Ali wiped a tear. Her father may have been stern, harsh even, but he was a rock. They never worried that there would be food on the table or a roof over their heads. He was tough, and he taught them to be, too. He was always there, whenever and for whatever they needed him.

She remembered, with shame, the anger she'd had at her mother for leaving, as though it was her choice to do so.

Enough. She was getting lost in the emotions of the last few days.

Ali opened the box and looked inside.

A slightly musty smell wafted in the air around it.

She carefully removed three large manilla envelopes and laid them on the table. They were all sealed with string wrapped around a cardboard disk. Ali had the urge to open them first but resisted. She decided to get it all out and then dive into each after the box was empty.

She gasped when she saw what was under the envelopes. A photo album!

As far as she knew, there was one lone picture of Joetta Bowles. It was that framed wedding day shot on the tea cart in the corner.

My goodness, what if these are more pictures of our beautiful mom?

There were Valentine's cards, thank you cards, and little notes. They were signed "JB." The "b" looked practically like calligraphy. Her mother's writing was so flowery and feminine that it was almost art.

Ali ran a hand over the puffy cover of the album but, again, set it next to the envelopes instead of opening it.

At the bottom of the box was a jewelry case.

Wow. Okay, jeez, Dad, if this is Mom's jewelry, why the heck wouldn't you have given it to us?

She was freshly annoyed with Bruce Kelly at that moment.

She lifted the blue jewelry box out and set it next to the rest of the items.

Two more artifacts made up the rest of the little treasure trove.

There was a mason jar. She picked it up, and dozens of little snow-white seashells shifted in the jar. *A souvenir from a long-ago beach vacation?*

Finally, the bottom of the box was wrapped in a deteriorating plastic dry-cleaning bag. Ali's emotions nearly knocked her over.

It was the dress! The wedding dress! A mini; so pretty, so modern for its day. Bruce had hung on to his dead wife's wedding dress.

She slid it out of the box and then placed the box on the floor. She *had* to see this dress.

The plastic bag fluttered to the kitchen floor, and she put her hands on the fabric. It was cream, not yellow. The photo made it seem yellow. It was so much more delicate than the picture, now fading, in the frame.

This dress was expensive. It was easy to see, to feel. In fact, Ali was quite sure she'd never held a garment this luxurious in feel. It was simply beautiful. A mock turtleneck and long sleeves gave it a modest vibe on top, and a paisley pattern in light caramel overlaid the ivory fabric and added interest without making it look too busy. A tiny fabric belt cinched the waist, and the more conservative top part of the dress contrasted with its length.

A mini! Ali still couldn't quite believe that.

The buttons were all covered and the stitching, the finishing, were clearly a higher quality than anything Ali had ever owned. Her mother looked so sweet in this dress. Ali had gazed at the picture a million times. And now it was in her hands!

Ali found the label: Miss Dior. *Was that Christian Dior? Wow!*

Another shocker. How did her mother afford this? She wondered if Joetta Bowles Kelly had thrifted it. What a detail to learn now, after this expanse of time, that her mother liked to find quality thrift pieces. Maybe she'd snagged it at a garage sale in nearby Ottawa Hills? Ali did have vague memories of walking the sidewalks with her mother at the exclusive and more well-to-do version of Old Orchard. It was just a few blocks away and could have yielded this treasure for her mother's wedding day. Ali's imagination was unlocked as she held the garment.

She looked at the label, size 2. Her mother was tiny.

That was it—the entire contents of the box. Ali wanted to dive into the album first to see the photos.

But then she stopped. It felt too much to do alone, too overwhelming.

This was, in fact, her sisters' mother, as well. Faye and Blair deserved to see this, too. They deserved to have this memory. Was it selfish to do this alone? She wished her sisters were here right now.

Ali kept the album shut and decided to move to the envelopes. Ali pulled out the first one. It was clearly all legal documents.

She read the heading. It was a law firm with a Florida address.

Dear Mr. Kelly....

In very formal legal jargon, the letter appeared to be discussing a property in Mangrove County, Florida.

Ali located her smartphone and plugged in the name of the county.

Okay, so it was on Florida's Gulf side, wedged between Manatee and Pinellas Counties. She'd never heard of Mangrove County, but all she really knew of Florida was Disney and Miami.

She wasn't a lawyer, but it looked like this letter was informing Bruce Kelly about several acres of "prime" beachfront real estate.

Was Dad trying to invest?

She slid the letter over to reveal several more legal-looking papers.

It was a deed.

The words "Haven Beach, Florida," were typed into the open lines of the documents.

Okay, so Dad owned land in Florida at one point? That did not seem like Bruce Kelly at all. But maybe you never really know your parents.

She scanned the deed, wishing she was more versed in law and real estate and all that.

Whatever this was, it was old. Decades and decades old.

She read through to the end and then saw it.

Did it mean what she thought it did?

Deeded, in perpetuity, to Ali Kelly, Faye Kelly, and Blair Kelly.

What?

She opened the next folder. In it were copies of more letters from this law firm.

Despite your refusal...

Held in trust....

Until such time as...

Bruce Kelly had filled this box with secrets. Ali was, in turn, curious and furious.

What mess was this? Was it long over? In perpetuity? That didn't sound over.

She picked up her phone.

"Hey, Faye. You need to get over here."

Seven

FAYE

"Sorry to hear about your dad."

"Thanks, Oscar. Thanks."

"Yeah, he was a tough SOB. Gotta love that old school about him."

She nodded. Oscar was right. Her dad was a tough SOB, she thought as she walked out of the plant after her shift.

Faye had made this walk every working day for the last twenty-nine years at Jeep.

It was so different from the now-demolished Parkway plant. That place had started as a bicycle factory. That plant was where Bruce had worked and Bruce's dad Chet, before that.

Boy were they chuffed when Faye had announced she was going to follow in their footsteps.

But she'd done it. And almost thirty years later, she was a valuable member of the team that assembled Jeep Wranglers.

These days, she didn't have to operate a machine or work a spot on the line anymore.

She also didn't have to rely on her skills as a tool and die maker. Ha, she hadn't used that hard-won skill in years. However, she was proud of it. She was a groundbreaker. And she knew it.

These days, Faye was valuable for what she knew, who she knew, and her knowledge of whether a problem was manageable without management.

And she knew how to talk to the guys.

That was her value. Institutional knowledge, they called it.

In the early days, Bruce Kelly's "getting her in" at the plant was a strike against her. It was a hurdle. Maybe, thanks to being his daughter, she had fewer gross comments from the guys, but then again, they just said stuff quieter, so Bruce didn't hear.

He was almost embarrassed that she'd gone into the trades. Old school that he was. But in the end, to his last breath, he'd said he was proud. That was something.

She'd started at the plant in 1996, but it may as well have been 1956. Her grandmother had worked on the line in the war, but somehow, that didn't translate to her generation. By high school, her dad was expecting her to do something more "girly."

But she hadn't. Bruce hadn't talked about his deceased wife, the girls' mother, but there was an undercurrent that not having a mom meant Faye didn't know what "girls" were supposed to do.

She hadn't worried about all that. She'd learned how to talk to the guys by knowing how to talk to Bruce Kelly. He was tough. But also not without charm. He could have been a bigger boss at Local 12, but he always said he didn't want to deal with all the drama. He was content to be a shop steward at different points.

Because it *was* drama. The inside of an auto plant was no different from any other workplace in that way.

Plus, there were plenty of other women here now. Though most of the ones she'd come up with were getting ready for retirement. Thirty and out. That was the goal.

Faye didn't know if it was *her* goal, but it was a mantra for a lot of them.

She'd met her husband here, worked until she was eight months pregnant here, and divorced her husband here.

The Jeep Plant had changed hands over the years; she started out on Parkway, and that place was gone. These days, she worked at the Toledo North Assembly Plant, where Jeep Wranglers rolled off the line. It was a massive complex, humming with activity and constantly in motion with production and deliveries. But it was also exclusive. While this was a huge employer in their region, you couldn't get inside unless you were supposed to be inside.

She was proud every time she saw a Wrangler on the road or in a movie. Or anywhere.

Faye didn't know if thirty and out was her plan. She did know it was a different kind of plant that had become her obsession.

Faye loved to garden. She loved it more than just about anything except her family.

She didn't mind working the second shift for that very reason. The daylight hours were hers to garden, weed, replant, rake, or do anything else her little patch of backyard seemed to need.

Faye had gone into this work, in part, to get Bruce Kelly's attention. It was a middle-child move. And now that he was gone, she wondered, what was worth her attention? What did she want to do?

She had the little inheritance from that tough SOB, her dad, and she had a good income here, and a paid-off ranch house in a cute neighborhood. She was going to use some of that inheritance to get a little backyard greenhouse. That could take her seed starting to a whole new level.

That idea was running through her mind when the phone buzzed at nearly midnight as she drove home from work.

"Hey, Faye. You need to get over here."

"Hey, sis. It's late. Is everything okay? You're usually long asleep by this hour."

"Yeah, I'm okay. It's okay, but I found something while I was cleaning out Dad's place. I think you need to come look."

"Now? Tonight?"

"No, it's not an emergency or anything. It's not life or death, but it's odd. Crazy even. And there are pictures I think we need to look at together."

"Odd like, Precious imprisoned in a secret hole in the basement, odd? Or odd, like dad has a secret collection of vintage dental floss?"

"Yeah, no, he's not a serial killer, and the only thing he collected was coffee cans of nails. Like, why? So many coffee cans of nails. But anyway, yeah, I want to run some paperwork I found by you. And brace yourself for this one: he's got a box of some of Mom's stuff he never showed us!"

That last part felt like a bombshell. Ali was underplaying it—but Mom's stuff!

"Oh wow. No way. Okay, I can do that; how about I bring a couple of bagels from Barry's for an early lunch? We can eat before I head to work."

"Perfect."

They ended the call. *Mom's stuff?* They just had that one picture. Faye had so little in her memory to hold onto when it came to their mom.

And this late call didn't do anything to alleviate Faye's worries about Ali. Usually, it was the other way around. Ali worried about Faye. Ali worried about Dad. Ali worried about Blair. But right now, Ali was making moves that were so out of character.

Was it Dad's death that had unmoored the order in Ali's life? Was it catching Ted in the act?

Ali had worked for years with very little praise and credit from their dad, and she'd replicated that with her husband and her boss. In Faye's eyes, Ali was the sun, and the people around her all paled in wattage. Ali didn't see it that way.

But now, her big sister, the responsible bedrock for all the Kelly Sisters, was making very drastic, un-Ali-like moves.

Faye pulled her car into the garage.

She was curious about the paperwork and what Ali found, but she was also tired. The death of their father was long, even though the funeral and services were short.

Maybe that was it. All the Kelly Sisters, from Ali to Blair and Faye in the middle, just needed a reset after a difficult year.

Faye got ready for bed and opened the book on container gardening she was reading.

She wanted to learn how to build a raised bed in her backyard before this spring. She was running out of space and needed to get creative.

Eight

ALI

Faye and Ali didn't eat the bagels Faye had procured. They were both too distracted, keyed up, and mesmerized by the box of stuff Ali had found.

Ali had gone up in the morning and found two more boxes. These were filled with expensive dresses, shoes, and bags.

"How in the heck did Mom afford this stuff?" Faye mused as they looked at the labels that read *Miss Dior, Pucci, Geoffrey Beene, Halston, Von Furstenberg*, and *Evan Picone*.

"No idea. I thought garage sale at first, but now? Well, they're all size two or four, so it would be really, really lucky for her to be able to thrift all in her size."

"And I mean, you've been to garage sales in Toledo. It's usually lawn equipment and creepy dolls. Do you remember her wearing fancy stuff?" Faye asked.

"No, I remember her being pretty, smelling pretty, but not wearing anything that stood out in the neighborhood. Right? She was just my mom."

After going through the dresses, Ali asked Faye if she wanted to look at the album.

Faye nodded, and the two of them sat side by side. The album had a green plastic cover.

This was why Ali had held back. If she was going to see her mother, she wanted to do it with her sisters.

At least one of them, anyway.

Ali carefully opened the cover. And there she was, Joetta Kelly, in lovely, petite blonde glory.

"Oh, that has to be you," Faye said, pointing to the baby in Joetta's arms.

"Wow, yeah, I'm sure. This looks very 1975, doesn't it?"

Their mother had a big hairpiece coiled on her head. Blonde, glamorous, and probably way too flashy for Bruce Kelly's vibe.

"Look at Dad, smiling. Wow, so he did know how," Faye quipped.

"Yeah, at least in the 1970s," Ali replied. And they laughed.

Their dad was handsome; she'd never thought of him that way. But in this yellowing photo, he clearly was. Maybe that's how he landed their mom, his square jaw and fit physique?

They turned the pages; they saw a similar posed shot for each of the girls. They were at the front door, with the house behind them. These were the first day or week back home after the hospital photos.

It is easy to forget that there was a time, not so long ago, when photos cost money. Bruce Kelly didn't have a camera that they knew of. What pictures they had back then must have been taken by someone else. And then he would have had to pay to have them developed. Ali had asked for a Kodak camera when she was in the fifth grade. She got it for Christmas.

"I'm taking photos of these photos right now to send to Blair." Faye snapped them with her cell phone.

"Maybe wait a second. Let's call her and warn her. We're together and can help each other process, and she's all by herself."

"True, true," Faye said. They turned another page.

They were around a Christmas tree.

And then another one.

"Oh my gosh!"

Faye was in diapers, and Ali was in a little red, white, and blue jumper. Their mom had both of them in her arms.

They turned the page again.

"What the heck is *this*?" Faye asked.

The fire hydrant was decorated to look like a minute man. The top was a blue hat, the body red and white striped.

"It's the bicentennial! Mom painted the fire hydrant like that. It was when I was a baby. Mom told me she did it."

Memories were clicking into Ali's mind. It was like a View-Master reel.

Click, Mom at the hydrant. Click, Mom, painting the bedroom. Click, broken glass. Broken glass?

"The fire hydrant that's out there, now, yellow?"

"Yes."

Click. Bruce, angry, painting over the minute man in bright yellow. Ali remembers crying then. Ali tried to tell her dad not to do that. She was more upset than when her mother died.

"Dad painted over it; I had forgotten all of that. He painted over it." Ali wiped away a tear. *Where was all this coming from?*

"Bruce sure wasn't one to let us sit in our feelings, was he?" Faye wrapped an arm around Ali, and for a moment, they both just processed the flood of memories and, worse, the lack of memories. It was hard to pin them down, these moments from their past.

Bruce hadn't let them see any of this stuff.

"Why do you think he did this, kept it all from us?" Faye asked.

"Well, probably what you said. Maybe he thought it was the best way for us to get on with it, as Dad liked to say."

"Right now, it is seeming rather cruel, don't you think?" Faye said.

Ali shrugged. Maybe it was cruel. Maybe it was all their dad knew how to do. It might have helped solidify those slippery scenes that faded in their minds. This was Mom's face, her hairdos, her hands. Ali had struggled to remember those things until she almost couldn't anymore.

"Let's give the photos a break—or maybe *I* need a break from them." Ali was feeling overwhelmed, more so than even the day their dad died.

"Yeah, agree. The boring legal stuff will snap us out of this. Nothing like legal documents to sober a party up," Faye said and reached for the pile of deeds.

Ali wondered about this propensity; they had to pull it together instead of crying. They were used to keeping their emotions under control. Did they know how to feel the grief that came with losing their parents? For sure, their dad did not want them to "cry like babies."

Ali and Faye laid out the documents from the envelopes. She read them again, and still the words seemed preposterous.

"If I'm reading this stuff right, we, the three of us, at some point, owned land in Florida," said Ali.

"Yeah, I mean, if Mr. Google is right, we had a nice spot on the beach. That would have been fun to know when I was looking for a place to go on spring break," joked Faye.

"Ha, yeah. So, it's probably nothing, but I haven't found anything that shows Dad or Mom sold it off. So, either they don't have the documentation in all this stuff or..."

"Ha, or we still own it," Faye finished her thought.

"I highly doubt that, but we need the lawyers to look at it, I think. We need to be sure everything's settled before we close out all of Dad's stuff." The estate had been straightforward up until this discovery.

"Agree. Did you call the lawyers?" They'd been using their dad's long-time law firm, Michalak, Perne, and Janco.

"Yes, I did. Louie asked me to scan it and send it over after we looked at it. I'll do that right after we dive into this. I think those dresses have value, so there may be something in there too that needs to be, uh, tallied." Ali pointed to the jewelry box.

"Nothing to do but open it," Faye said.

That was the last thing. The only thing they hadn't cracked open yet.

"Well, you ready? Maybe the Hope Diamond is in there?"

"Yeah, right, maybe so," Faye said.

But they understood each other. Finding all this had been like exposing their nerve endings. It was impossible to protect yourself from the past when it was now exploding all around them. And what they remembered didn't match at all with what they were looking at.

A vibrant life, their mother's, had ended too soon, and their father had decided to hide it all away from the daughters so desperately in need of some connection to her.

Ali was trying to suppress her anger. But she was mad at the man who'd done so much, so quietly, to keep their family together. Her anger had nowhere to land. Their dad was gone. Their mother, too. She rubbed her face with both her hands. She needed to reset to something less raw. Ali took a deep breath.

"Okay, open it," Ali said.

Faye did as she asked, slowly.

The midday light from the kitchen window caught the contents of the jewelry box just right.

Sparkle, color, and even a strand of pearls made it seem like they'd opened a pirate's treasure chest.

"Wow," Faye said.

"Yeah, Joetta Kelly had a lot of bling."

Bling was an understatement.

Nine

ALI

A few days later, Ali and Faye sat down in front of Louie Michalak of Michalak, Perne, and Janco.

The law firm handled just about every UAW member in Toledo. A few days ago, they'd thought this was an open and shut estate to settle. Well, it was all back open again, thanks to Ali's attic discoveries.

The offices were the opposite of posh. In fact, you could still faintly smell cigarette smoke that had to be embedded into the fibers of the orange couch in Louie's office. The place was as old school as it got. Fake wood paneling, dusty books lining the walls, and carpets that were remnants of the swinging '70s took you back in time. Ali imagined this place had looked new about a decade before she was born.

But it was just this frozen-in-time *Goodfellas* vibe that kept clients like Bruce comfortable. Toledo's seven thousand Jeep employees meant there was always work to be done at Michalak, Perne, and Janco. If you had an issue, someone at the plant would tell you about this firm. It was located on Lagrange Street, an easy drive for anyone who worked at the now-demolished old Jeep plant. Ali realized she had never actually seen Janco but assumed he was rattling around here somewhere.

Ali and Faye laid out all the paperwork they'd found and provided pictures of the jewelry and couture clothing.

"I did some research, and my friend is a jewelry appraiser, and well, we're looking at about ten thousand dollars, give or take, worth of jewelry," Ali told the attorney, who'd been verifying the documents they'd found.

"And I handled some initial research on the dresses," Faye added. "That's at least five grand, maybe ten, of high fashion rags Bruce was hiding in the garage attic."

These ballpark numbers were staggering to Ali. Ten to twenty thousand dollars of vintage, high-quality pieces languishing in the garage attic. It was bizarre and didn't seem real.

"Probably a miracle they weren't full of moth holes," remarked Louie.

"I don't know. Dad kept a pretty tight ship," Ali replied.

"Okay, so do we need to do anything about amending the value of the estate or something?" Faye said, cutting to the chase.

Ali needed that. Normally, she was so efficient. She was usually the one shooting in to get it done. But these boxes, these secrets her dad kept, along with everything else, had her unmoored.

"No. If the three of you agree to sell them, just split the proceeds three ways, it's all the same as the house and pension and all that," Louie explained. "It's this...this is the thing that's a bit of a mess." Louie pointed a gnarled finger at the paperwork.

"How so?" Faye asked.

"This is legitimately the title of six structures and a condo or some such multi-room unit in Haven Beach, Florida in Mangrove County. I can't find any recent sales or documentation on it. No transfers on it."

"So, who owns this? Dad?" Ali asked. But she knew her

father's name was nowhere on any of the documents. She didn't have an ounce of legal training, but she could read. She just hadn't believed what she read.

"Our research indicates that no, your dad didn't own it. You three girls own it. It's in your names and Blair's. You've always owned it—or have since the early '80s."

Ali took a deep breath.

"I also researched the addresses," Louie continued. "They are legit, and this appears to be a good location. Which could be very nice."

"Or it's like that thing where someone bought land in the Everglades scam." Ali felt that was a more likely scenario.

"No, it's not the Everglades. It is beachfront on the Gulf, but any more than that, I can't tell you. There's a management company listed as the contact for these addresses, but no one has returned my calls."

"What's your advice on this, Louie?" Ali asked.

"My advice? Go down there and see what you've got. The number isn't working, like I said. And the only way to know what it actually is would be to get eyes on it."

"We can sell it, though, right?" Faye asked. Ali saw a little light in her sister's eyes. She was sure Faye was mentally adding wings to her backyard greenhouse plan with this money.

"Again, you'd all have to agree to sell. It's a shared property, or one would have to buy out the other two kind of thing," Louie explained.

"Do we have to do anything?" Ali asked.

"Well, technically, yes, you would owe taxes. I haven't been able to figure out how this hasn't been an issue yet, but anyway, now that you know..."

"It's our mess to clean up, whatever it is," Ali finished for him.

"Yes. If you want me to continue to handle it, I can make some calls to an attorney in Jacksonville. That's the closest referral I have."

Ali knew then, out of the blue, exactly what she was going to do. This was her next project. She was going to close out her father's—or her mother's—estate. As the oldest sister, she saw it as her duty.

"No, we'll handle it, Louie. Thank you for verifying all this."

Ali stood up. Faye followed suit. Old Louie Michalak had to use the desk to assist in the effort of standing up.

"Let me know if you need me to do anything else. Tell Tami Lou out front, and she's got my schedule if you have any more questions. Otherwise, the check for the house, well, divide by three, and you're all set."

"Thanks."

"And again, sorry for your loss. Bruce was good people, one of my first clients right after your mom passed."

All this reminded Ali that she probably needed someone in the firm to deal with her separation from Ted. It had receded to the back burner as this little kettle boiled.

"Thanks, Louie."

Tami Lou was on the phone as they walked through the reception area, but she waved goodbye to them. Ali would have to give her a call.

The sisters made their way out to the parking lot. Faye looped her arm through Ali's. It was freezing today and walking across the law office parking lot felt like crossing a frozen tundra. The wind was kicking up, and the fine powdery snow over the icy parking lot made each step treacherous. They helped each other toward Ali's Jeep.

"Penguin it," Ali said. And they both did their best imitation of penguins as they got to the car without slipping. Barely.

Ali got in and started the engine.

"You'd think the lawyers would salt better out here, jeez," Faye groaned.

"Yeah." The cold had permeated into Ali's bones in the brief trek from office to Jeep. She punched the heat to maximum as the Jeep idled.

"Well, that was, uh, interesting," Faye said.

"Yeah, it was." Ali was making mental plans on how to get the information they needed about the Florida property.

"Can I run something by you, Ali?"

"Of course." Ali put her fingers up to her face and huffed her warm breath into them to try to break the brittle chill.

"I don't want to sell Mom's stuff, not yet anyway."

Ali knew what she meant; it was a connection. Something their long-dead mother owned, touched, and loved. And they'd only just found it. "I don't want to either." Ali was relieved that Faye felt the same. This wasn't about the money at all.

"I know Blair probably needs the cash," Faye said. "I could probably use it too, but with the house sale, I have a little cushion, and I just—"

Ali stopped her and put a hand on Faye's. "I get it. We have a little window into Mom, and we don't want to close it."

"Right."

"Okay, but you heard Louie, we all need to decide. And if say, Blair says, no, let's get liquid, we can figure something out. We for sure can hang on to the jewelry and dresses for a little while. I have no idea about the property. But yeah, I want to hang on to, to—"

"To Mom," Faye said.

"Yes."

"Okay. What about the swamp land in Florida situation?"

"I don't know. That's a tougher nut. Seems very, uh, tangled up. But I'm thinking something about that, too. Let me think a little more. We can always have Louie call his guy in Jacksonville if we can't handle this ourselves."

"Yeah, okay. Well, I need to get to work. Can you drive me home?"

"Yep, call Blair, put her on speaker. We'll get her up to speed."

Ten

DIDI

It had been a busy morning. It was funny, what constituted busy to her these days. They'd had one appointment for Jorge and then gone to the hardware store. She wanted a nap now. That would have been nothing in her forties or even fifties and sixties. But something about being in her seventies was, as the kids say, hitting different.

She wanted to zonk out for a bit, but alas. No time for that!

Didi and Jorge lived in a condo a few blocks away from Sea Turtle Resort.

They used to be able to stroll over here from their condo, easy peasy.

She just had to walk along Bayview a short way to where it ended a block from the Sea Turtle. She could get her steps in and check on guests in one quick walk! Plus, Jorge was never more than a few minutes wait for any maintenance issue that popped up when they weren't here.

It was such a good retirement setup for both of them. Well, it used to be.

And today's news hadn't been what they wanted to hear.

"He is not to lift anything that weighs more than a gallon of milk, got it?" Doctor Diller had instructed them.

"I told you that." Didi had smacked Jorge on the shoulder.

"Hey, I'm in recovery."

"I told him not to try to get the chlorine out of the shed, but what does he do?"

"You can't lift it, not with your frozen shoulder."

"Ugh, the two of us barely make one complete functioning human!"

The doctor had written something on his prescription pad.

"Look, you both need PT."

"What? I didn't have surgery! He's the one with a new hip."

"Yes, but your shoulder could stand some physical therapy. Or we could do surgery on you too." Doctor Diller had looked over his readers at both of them.

They did not have time for another surgery right now.

"Fine, fine. Therapy," Didi had said.

She'd taken the script and another for antibiotics, so Jorge's infection stayed gone.

Jorge had waited in the truck while she picked up laundry soap and bleach for the resort. Then he'd done nothing but complain as she tried to get it from the truck to the shed.

"Let me help you at least get it on the hand cart."

Between the two of them, they'd unpacked the truck and now were ready for said nap.

It was barely one in the afternoon.

Jorge sat uncomfortably in the chair opposite the little desk they had in the complex's office space. The space functioned as a check-in desk, a laundromat for the guests, and their office. This place, too, was in disarray. There just wasn't time to organize here and do the pool and keep up with the guests. However, Didi realized they didn't have many guests lately. That, she decided, was a blessing. Fully booked would be too much to handle right now.

"Ugh, the air conditioning fan is busted. That's why it's making that noise."

Didi hadn't noticed. What she had noticed was the pile of bills. "What are we going to do with these?"

"Well, what's the account looking like?"

"It's a little thin," Didi told him. "Our last guest on the cottages left in a huff, if you recall."

"We have two families coming for cottages, so that should be enough to handle that little pile."

"I can always dip into our—"

"No," Jorge interrupted. "We said no to that. If this place doesn't fly anymore, we agreed, no life support."

"I am not ready to pull the plug on Sea Turtle. I'm not. We're just going to have to get better, you and me."

"No argument here. I told you it's your call, and this place is our retirement hobby as long as you want to do this. I will say I'm sick of being in here though. What about we take the chairs out to the beach?"

"Yeah, that sound is annoying. But I carry the chairs, mister." The chairs were resin, light weight, and Didi knew for a fact she could carry two without too much trouble.

Jorge harrumphed at her declaration. Then he stood up and walked over to the air conditioning unit. He banged the side of it with his hand. It was a wall unit that kept the office cool. Central air in their office was wasteful, plus they were barely in here. Most of their work was out with the guests, on the grounds, in the motel. This place was a phone and files and the attached laundry. The smack to the side of the air conditioning unit did the trick. It stopped moaning in protest.

Didi thought about the phone. Her wandering cell phone. She just hadn't ever adjusted to using it like a landline. Thinking about the landline, she reshuffled the pile of bills.

There it was. This had to be the reason they'd had a few quiet weeks of rentals.

Past due from the Tampa Telecomm.

"Oh no, that was one of the bills I neglected! The phone! It's not on!"

"No wonder bookings are down," Jorge sighed. "No one can call. Good thing you're a bombshell. Otherwise, I'm sure I'd have no use for you."

Didi slid herself under Jorge's shoulder to steady him. She could see the effort it was taking him to stand up and tinker with the air conditioner.

"Oh, yes, thank goodness for that. How else did I snag the Latin Lover of Mangrove County?" She rolled her eyes at the comment.

"Let me put the check to the phone company in the slot, and we'll head out to the water."

"Perfect."

Ten minutes later, they were in their spots.

Somehow, Jorge managed to find two clean beach towels in the towel caddy and draped them over the resin chairs. Oops, another thing Didi needed to tend to. She needed to gather the towels, launder them, and restock them. The list kept getting longer.

"Get that in our mail slot?"

"I did. Yes, the phone should be back in service in a day or two." She knew most people paid bills on the internet. But she didn't trust the internet. She mailed the bills in...well, when she remembered.

"Good, good. Now, let's just relax. We don't want to miss it."

"When you're right, you're right."

As they settled into their chairs, their friend Henry showed up with wine.

Henry owned the cutest little beach restaurant, the Seashell Shack. He couldn't make the scene every day, but today was their lucky day. He must have sensed they needed a little something good to end the day.

"What? You don't need to bring us libations, Henry Hawkins."

"Yeah? Well, I missed you two yesterday. I thought I'd check on my favorite love birds."

"Oh, you're too sweet," Didi said.

Henry Hawkins was Henry Handsome in her book. He had the look of Timothy Olyphant, Didi's favorite from that show *Deadwood* that Jorge liked. Jorge teased her that Henry was her backup plan. Maybe if she was twenty years younger!

Sure, Henry was thoughtful and handsome, but what she loved about Henry—and a few other owners here on this stretch of Haven Beach really—was that he got it. He wanted to hold the line with them.

The small mom-and-pop owners on Haven Beach stuck together because there weren't many places in Florida left run by mom or pop, or Henry, as the case may be.

Big companies with names like General Capital Group, or Starworth LLC, or Sterling Industries owned most condos or restaurants. She wondered if there were any other places like Sea Turtle. The Florida they grew up in had mostly disappeared, she feared.

"I'm sweet? Flattery will get you a heavy pour of the wine!"

They both raised their glasses, and Henry poured for the three of them.

Henry sat in the sand. He was fit and, in his fifties, he was still young enough to get up and down off the ground. Didi probably could, but Jorge? No way right now.

In about twenty minutes, they'd probably be wishing for long sleeves, but right now, January in Florida, sunset was just warm enough to sit in t-shirts and be comfortable.

Didi let the view do what it did for her soul: calm it, center it. The horizon in front of them made her feel small, or rather, like her everyday worries were small. They were all a part of a great big world, and the phone bill or the laundry were tiny specks of nothing in the scheme of things. She felt the tension leave her body and looked at the sky.

The sun was bright orange, but the sky was pink.

"Oh, it's a good one," Jorge said.

Nearly every evening, they did this; sometimes just the two of them, sometimes their fellow Haven Beach residents joined them. When the complex was full, families, newlyweds, and every type of guest did the same.

Every sunset was different here. But each was beautiful.

Didi shifted in her chair. The fact was her worries were stronger than the laundry or a sunset. They weren't dissolving fully, as they had in past seasons. She loved this life here. But they were in trouble. If they didn't get some help or get stronger, they wouldn't be able to keep Sea Turtle going. She needed a solution. Things had to change.

Jorge reached for her hand. He knew she was fretting, even though she hadn't said a word.

His hand on hers calmed her. That was the important thing. The two of them. Their family.

This would all work out.

"What can possibly be wrong when you're looking at this view?"

"Amen, Didi, amen," Henry replied.

She hoped Jorge would be stronger tomorrow. She had to have faith that they'd come up with a solution for all the work that needed to be done here.

Didi had no idea that the Law Firm of Louie Michalak of Michalak, Perne, and Janco had called half a dozen times only to hear the message that their phone wasn't connected.

Eleven

ALI

An overnight stop in North Georgia was all she needed. Ali had made the drive by herself in two days, spending one night at the Hampton Inn.

She'd experienced the wonder of Buc-ees in Richmond, Kentucky, and the terror of a sketchy 2 am, ill-selected rest stop in Tennessee. But she'd crossed the state line in Florida at 5 pm, and as she traveled toward the Gulf and Mangrove County, there was still a little daylight to go.

On day two, she'd traded her oversized turtleneck and leggings for a cotton blouse and, well, leggings. But she was able to fold up her down-filled parka and shove it under her suitcases in the back of the Jeep.

"No need to see you for a few days!"

The warm air in February was a novelty. She was so used to being frozen to the bone. She was so used to layers and having to scurry to get back inside this time of year. But here, even at the gas station, she was taking deep breaths and embracing the air instead of bracing against it.

"Why do I live where the air hurts again?" she asked no one in particular.

I-75 was easy, but as she neared Haven Beach, she gripped her steering wheel and turned her music down so she could hear the signs. Sure, that was an oxymoron, but she didn't want to get lost. Ali followed the GPS instructions. US-41, Tamiami Trail, Manatee County, each road getting smaller and slower.

After she crossed over the Manatee River, she really started to feel the difference between driving around Tampa or Orlando and what it felt like here. Could the ocean call you? It felt like that was happening. Or else she just had been behind the wheel too long and needed to stretch her legs. Maybe both were true.

Ali had never been to this side of Florida. Bruce had no time for family vacations, and Ted insisted all their vacations were to visit "historical" sites. In his philosophy, the kids should learn something while on break. They couldn't do that at Wally World, as he liked to call the entire state of Florida.

Ali wished she would have pushed; she knew both her kids loved Disney movies. But they'd never given them that as kids.

Maybe someday with the grandkids? Grandkids? Was that next? Ali had a lot to sort out before she went shopping for a grandma name. She had been to Orlando, on a conference, and once in college, Daytona. But this gulf side was new to her.

One beach after another stretched before her. She knew she was supposed to take Gulf Boulevard Drive. Hang a right. To the left, she'd be on Long Boat Key, to the right, Haven Beach, and if she went too far, she'd fall off the barrier island into the Atlantic.

Haven Beach was the tip of the strip, according to her map.

She wondered why she'd never heard of it. Although she had not been to this part of Florida, many of her Toledo friends had, from St. Pete to Treasure Island.

Haven Beach though? She'd never seen vacation pics or family portrait sessions from the place. It worried her a bit; what would she find?

Ali had booked a hotel room online at the Marriott Courtyard. The sun was setting, and she didn't want to go to the property they allegedly owned in the dark. She didn't know what she would find, but whatever it was, daylight was a better proposition than night.

Her hotel was across Gulf Boulevard. It was clean, easy to find, and she'd accumulate a few hotel points by booking it. Ali was tired, and her body ached a bit from gripping the steering wheel for two days straight.

She'd hauled in her small bag and sat on the hotel bed. It was almost dusk, but she wanted to be outside. She had the urge to stretch her legs a little. Maybe she'd just walk along Gulf Boulevard a bit and find a bite to eat.

She was still in leggings and a tunic, but every person she'd seen here had flip-flops on and shorts or a sundress. She didn't own a single sundress. And her legs were whiter than the snow she'd left behind. Leggings it was. She switched out the tunic for a Mud Hens t-shirt. This was hardly fun-in-the-sun chic, but she wasn't really on vacation either. She was on a mission.

By the time she'd changed, the sun had already gone down, though it wasn't dark yet. Something about the vibe here was so different from any other place she'd been in this state.

The idea of donning a conference I.D. lanyard or getting in line for a ride? Nope. The vibe was flip-flop.

Ali grabbed her wallet and phone and double-checked that she had a room key. She'd just walk a little to loosen the stiffness in her bones.

The air was different here. She could almost taste the salt! And the congestion she'd seen along Gulf, at other points on the trip, had slowed to a trickle. There were only a few cars going back and forth as she used the crosswalk to get to the beach side of the road.

At first, she couldn't put her finger on what made this little stretch of road different, but it started to dawn on her as she walked. There weren't any high-rise condos.

Almost every square inch of road on both sides along the coast, there were huge condo complexes five stories or more high. She supposed it made sense. It was to pack in as many vacationers or timeshares or whatever.

Here, there were condos, for sure, but also beach houses that weren't brand new. Or if they were brand new, they were made to look lived in.

It felt cozy here. That seemed ridiculous. Skeptically, she wondered if it had been designed to make her feel like that by some Disney-esque Imagineer.

Ali had walked for about ten minutes when she realized she ought to probably turn around and head back to her room. But then an aroma caught her and seemed to pull her toward it.

She realized all she'd eaten in the last two days was food from gas stations and drive-throughs. The smell reminded her that an actual meal, sitting at a table would be a good idea.

She followed her nose, or her stomach, to the source. Several weathered wooden planks nailed to a post pointed the way—or rather, pointed the way for several options. On top of the sign sat an odd assortment of seashells for decoration. Ali decided to follow the painted red arrow that pointed from the parking lot to a small restaurant, which was conveniently right on the beach.

When in Rome, thought Ali, *eat on the beach*.

She did as the sign instructed: *This way to the Seashell Shack*.

There was a decided lack of gloss in this little stretch of Florida, and it turned out the Seashell Shack was aptly named. The restaurant had the trappings of a beachy shack, all weathered boards and sandy floors, but it was also fresh, clean, and inviting. A wall of windows looked out to the water, and beyond that, Ali could see a patio and the beautiful beach.

This will do just fine!

Ali also hoped they were still serving something. She'd noticed more people were heading out than in at the fairly early time of 6:30 pm.

But no one stopped her, so she walked further into the Seashell Shack. She continued through toward the porch. She was itching to take off even her flip-flops and get in the sand.

This really was seaside.

The smallest picnic table was a four-top and Ali felt a little guilty taking one all by herself. In fact, she felt a little self-conscious about having dinner at a restaurant on her own. For so long, she'd had a family of four, or Ted, or some combination of her sisters as dining companions.

A tall but broad busboy in beat-up jeans had his back to Ali as he cleared a table. She'd just ask, to make sure it was okay.

"Excuse me, is it seat yourself?"

The busboy turned around, and it turned out to be more of a bus "man." A man with salt and pepper hair, similarly hued scruff on his chin, and a fair amount of smile lines turned his friendly face in her direction.

"Well, the floorshow is over, so yes. You're welcome to whatever table suits you. Though, there is a breeze; maybe one there on the corner to get a little shelter from the wind?"

Ali found herself smiling back. If this was what bussers looked like on Haven Beach, maybe she needed to rethink the length of her stay.

"I appreciate it, thank you."

"I let some of my waitresses go early, so get settled and I'll be out with a menu. How about our signature drink? You have a look of up north to you. Our job here is to help you shake that off."

Ali hadn't been thinking of cocktails when she wandered in, but then again, she also hadn't expected to be gob-smacked like a teenager by a middle-aged busboy. They made them handsome here in Haven Beach.

Though, wait, what did he say? He let his servers go. Maybe he's the manager?

73

She found herself nodding in agreement, and he put an arm out toward the table he'd recommended.

Ali sat at the table and realized he was right; the breeze was a little chilly, but the side of the building blocked it a bit. She should have brought a sweater.

She looked out at the water. There were people enjoying beer, finishing baskets of fish, and just relaxing here at the Seashell Shack.

Relaxing. That was something she had a hard time with. Ali reminded herself this wasn't a vacation; it was a fact-finding mission. She needed to figure out where this property was and how to unload it.

But plenty of time for that tomorrow.

Right now, food.

The salt and pepper manager returned. On top of his faded jeans, he wore a t-shirt with the same Seashell Shack logo she'd seen on the sign outside. He had a menu in one hand and a bright orange drink in the other. It looked fruity.

"This is the patented Seashell Shack Daq."

"Daiquiri?"

"In that same neighborhood." He handed her the menu, which was one sheet laminated and printed on both sides.

"Can you tell me what that wonderful smell is?"

"Ah, yes, that's our Key Lime dessert. Normally, the fresh seafood draws our newbies, but that pie just came out of the oven."

"I'd love that, but I suppose I should have a dinner. Diabetes isn't the greatest choice for my visit."

"Ah, well, how about this?" He pointed to crab cakes and coleslaw, and she nodded. "My menu is simple, not much to choose from, but what we do, we do really well."

"Okay then, dinner it is. Hold off on the pie."

"Come on, live a little, Mud Hen."

Ali looked down at her t-shirt. Someone always said something when they saw that logo.

"I guess so. Pie, too."

"My name's Henry, by the way. I own the place. If you need anything, I'm your man. On that note, hang on—"

Henry disappeared, and Ali looked around. She smiled. She was sort of surprised, as nice as the owner was and as great as the food smelled, that it really was deserted so early.

Henry returned and offered her something that was not on the menu. "Here, take this sweatshirt from our little gift shop. You really aren't dressed right for the beach now that the floorshow is over." He handed her a sweatshirt with the same logo as the t-shirt he wore.

"You said that before. Is there a band or entertainment?"

"Every evening, the greatest show on Earth. It's winter so tonight it was 6:00 pm. Tomorrow a little later."

He put his arm out to the horizon. She looked out to the ocean. A couple people were strolling, and a few kids were still running on the beach, but mostly, it was quiet.

"The ocean is your floorshow?"

"Actually, the sunset. You came just a touch too late for it today. But you can catch it tomorrow, our Grand Finale."

"Ah, well, that's a lot more family-friendly than I usually associate with floorshow."

"Yeah, just a joke. So you from Toledo, or just a *M*A*S*H* fanatic?"

"From Toledo, born and raised. Go Hens."

"Go Hens. I hear you have a nice new baseball stadium. I played in the old one, Ned Skeldon, I think they called it?"

"Yes, well, we've had the new one for over twenty years, but I remember the old one, The Ned."

"Yeah, my very short, very non-illustrious career had me in your fair city one summer."

Ali couldn't believe the coincidence and said as much.

"Yeah, except everyone down here has some connection to up there. It's crazy."

"Ah."

"Now, you get your Shack Daq in you, and you'll be on beach time by the time I bring out the crab cakes and pie." He winked at her.

Oh, wow, what a charmer, she thought. From busboy to restaurant manager to owner to former baseball player. Ali figured he must have quite the story.

She watched as Henry disappeared into the restaurant.

Ali didn't know what beach time was, but she did know that, even with the little breeze, this was lovely.

Her phone buzzed; she looked down. The news app on her phone let her know that it was a First Alert Snow Advisory in Toledo.

She took a sip of her Shack Daq and let the cold drink warm her from the inside out.

Twelve

ALI

She'd made it an early evening. The food, the fresh key lime pie, and the Shack Daq had her sleepy and ready to turn in.

Ali had wanted to return the sweatshirt to Henry, but he'd insisted on letting her keep it.

"Please add this to my bill," she'd tried to insist.

"Free advertising for me. You're a model, right?"

She'd rolled her eyes. "Yes, a five-foot three-inch model pushing fifty. I rarely get out of bed for under ten thousand dollars."

"I figured." Henry had laughed easily.

That was rare, finding a new person with the same sense of humor. But this wasn't Ali's first rodeo. She could spot a shameless flirt a mile away. But it was still nice to be flirted with now and then.

Despite the strength of the Shack Daq, it was just the right potion to give Ali a relaxed sleep. With work, Ted, and then her father, she wasn't sure when she'd slept without a million interrup-

77

tions. Sure, she had a potty break, but that's midlife. She had to accept that.

The weather app called for a high in the low seventies and sunshine, but with a possibility of an afternoon thunderstorm.

Ah, Florida. Wasn't that the forecast every day?

Ali decided her legs were too white for shorts, so she opted for her most comfortable jeans, and this time a plain white t-shirt and her platform Chuck Taylor's. She had good Chucks and knock around Chucks in her car. She opted for the knock-arounds that she didn't worry about keeping white.

Something told her that the state of the plot of land they owned had to be rough. Really rough, or why else wouldn't someone have tried to sell it? If it was anything but scrub or a garbage heap, why hadn't their dad tried to vacation there?

That alone told her she was about to encounter some sort of real estate albatross.

Ali got in her Jeep, plugged the address in, and did as Waze instructed.

"Turn right on Gulf Boulevard. In 1/8 of a mile, your destination will be on the left."

"Okay, so I could have walked," she replied to Waze. Ali and Waze were now best friends after driving around Atlanta during rush hour together.

She traveled a few numbers past the Seashell Shack.

"You've reached your destination."

But it came up on Ali so fast that she went past it. Waze began to get a real attitude about her stopping, turning around, and getting back on track.

"Okay, okay!"

Waze was a crappy best friend.

She pulled into a little grocery parking lot and then turned right to try to get to her target address.

A small oval sign, more weathered than even the Seashell Shack sign, dangled from a post. There was a cartoon turtle, a wave, and the greeting, *Welcome to Sea Turtle Resort*.

"Okay, well, this has to be it."

"Like I said," Waze replied.

Well, that's what she imagined Waze would say.

Ali pulled into a gravel covered and unkept front parking area. Her Jeep was the only vehicle in the parking lot. Overgrown palm trees, tropical plants of some variety, and—*what were they called? Mangrove?* They all seemed to be trying to overtake the space. She clicked the fob of her Jeep.

A paint-chipped little office building indicated that this was the right address. She had no idea what she'd find. Or if it was even inhabited.

She walked to the screen door and opened it. Inside were four washers and four dryers. None in rotation at the moment. To the right of that a counter, behind that, another door.

There was a vending machine with what appeared to be ancient food items and dusty beverages.

"Oh, man, this is the lobby at the motel at the end of the world," she said under her breath.

There was no sign of a manager or a clerk, and she was surprised that there was even this much of a structure here.

She looked at a map on the wall behind the counter.

It was an arc of small cottages arranged in a half circle, each with a cute little name. There was also a hook and key on each image of a cottage.

"You've got to be kidding me."

Ali walked back out of the office. She walked further into the overgrowth, half expecting the swamp thing to come out and grab her.

After navigating a trellis-type entrance, she couldn't believe her eyes. As the map depicted, there were six cottages in various states of disrepair.

Cottages? On the beach? Did they even have those in Florida anymore? She figured this explained why the was property was in their name. It was a white elephant or something. *Maybe they were built out of asbestos?*

The cottages were wood-shingled and covered in a variety of peeling paint colors. She spied yellow, red, lime, orange, pink, and blue!

There was a little courtyard that led out toward the ocean. She followed a path of stones partially obscured by sand. As she walked, no fewer than three little geckos skittered to and fro.

It wasn't long before the overgrown tropical vegetation cleared enough to see the sandy beach. Sea Turtle Resort might be dilapidated, but if it wasn't on a sinkhole or a haunted graveyard, maybe they could sell it and make quite a bit. The location alone was stunning!

For a moment, Ali was still, quiet. She was pulled into the scene in front of her. She was surprised by how she felt. This felt both new and familiar.

The sound of the waves rolling onto the sand, the caw of a pair of seagulls, and even the wind rustling through the palm fronds behind her entered her heart like music. Or rather, it was some aural frequency tuned to the base of her brain that vibrated down to the middle of her chest.

Her mind quieted, her breath got slower and deeper, and the air in her lungs was there on purpose.

Was it the water? The salty air? The warm wind after so many years of frigid winters?

She longed to take her shoes off and sink into the sand, as though it were the missing element of her biology. The entire experience made her feel...what was it? Grounded?

Ali didn't have time to process this before a voice floated over the sound of the waves.

"Don't forget to exhale."

The voice was also familiar. Had she heard it before?

Was it in her head? She did as the voice instructed and exhaled.

"Happens to me every day. Easy to gasp at the sight."

This wasn't in Ali's head. She turned to find a woman about her height, maybe in her seventies, standing a few feet behind her, hands on hips, head tilted to the side.

She had white hair piled in a chaotic nest on top of her head. She wore cargo shorts that stopped just below her knee, but the portion of her legs that they did reveal was tanned and toned. She wore a t-shirt that had the logo of the Sea Turtle Resort on the front and a chambray shirt over that. In her hand was a toolbox. And in her eyes, mirth. They were blue, inquisitive, and surrounded by gorgeous laugh lines—and those eyes were searching hers.

"Hello, I'm Didi, the uh, the manager here. I don't have any reservation arrivals listed for today, though Jorge and I have been a little scatterbrained lately. No worries if you're checking in today. I can get Key Lime ready for you. It's open and the closest to the beach."

"Ah, no, I'm not checking in. I'm here to assess the situation."

"Ah, the situation is sun and sand, as always."

"Uh, no," Ali said, "with the manager. I need the situation—or rather, I have questions about that."

"Oh well, that situation is, Jorge and I are getting on, and I must stop him from trying to vacuum the pool until his hip surgery fully heals. So, I apologize for being at Sixes and Sevens. You didn't talk to Karen Ort, did you? We did our best, but—"

"I, no, I'm not a guest. My name is Ali Harris, and it appears I own this place."

The woman took a sharp intake of air, and then lifted her hand to her mouth. It was her turn to be bowled over, it appeared. Didi blinked as if she wasn't sure if she was seeing things. She dropped the metal toolbox to the ground. It landed with a loud metallic clang.

Ali was slightly worried she'd caused Didi to have a stroke or something

"I think it's your turn to exhale." Ali stepped forward and put a gentle hand on the woman's arm. *Is she okay?*

Didi did as Ali instructed and exhaled. She shook her head and blinked. "Oh, wow, goodness, the ugh, management company, uh, they didn't tell us that. Well, it's just a surprise. I'd have prepared. We'd have done more, ugh, well, just...the laundry isn't even up to speed, Ali." The older woman appeared to be out of breath.

Did I come on too strong? Why is she so upset? Ali tried to bring the temperature down on the surprisingly fraught exchange.

"Honestly, I'm not here to grade the place or check-in. I'm here to figure out how this place wound up in my name and my sisters' names."

"Well, three on a deed, that's not unusual, is it?" Didi continued to search Ali's face.

Ali got a little self-conscious. *Do I have broccoli in my teeth or something?*

"What's unusual is that we had no idea we owned it, and it appears we have for a long time." She probably shouldn't spill these details to this stranger, but the woman was safe to talk to. Ali knew immediately.

"Really, well, uh, we just run it. I mean, we're not *in charge* in charge, so I can't help you there. In fact, never met the owners. Until now."

Ali shook her head. That didn't make sense.

"Who pays you? What's the name of the company?"

"Oh, Jorge handles that. We just manage the cottages, six of them here, and of course, the Inn."

"The Inn?"

"Yes, Sea Turtle is a resort property that includes that building right there. Six hotel rooms, each can accommodate a family of four! And the penthouse! Though, we're empty right now. No new calls these last two weeks because, uh...well, I have phone issues."

"Your phone is off."

"You figured that out, eh? I wish I had."

Ali hesitated. *Should I keep sharing? Is this woman's job in jeopardy now that I've arrived?* She plowed ahead, hoping she wasn't some sort of Ebenezer Scrooge in this current scenario. She should have realized that a change in management or ownership or whatever was happening here would worry the staff. Ali felt bad for being so blunt in her first encounter with this nice lady.

"We—that is, my attorney—called for two weeks. The phone is disconnected."

"Yeah, we just, uh, realized. It slipped through the cracks. I'm so sorry. Payment is on the way."

"Yeah, out of service." Ali bent down and picked up the toolbox. It was heavy. This little elderly lady shouldn't be hauling it around, she decided.

"Let's go in and have a spot of lemonade," Didi said, recovered somewhat. "We seem to have a lot to talk about."

"Yes. Good, yes. I have questions."

They turned from the water and back toward the cottages.

The woman seemed a tad bit shaky the first few steps but got her bearings and was soon confidently leading Ali back to the office building she had first explored.

The questions piled up in Ali's head by the dozens, and soon, the question of how Didi knew there were three Kelly sisters was replaced by ten others.

It would take more than one cold glass of lemonade to sort this out.

Thirteen

1974
Belinda

The Gulfside Girls, as they were called by just about everyone, sat on the beach together like they'd done just about every day the last few weeks.

The sisters' love of this beach started when they were tiny. It was one of Belinda Bennett's first memories.

Their grandparents owned the cottages and brought them here to play. Grandpa did grownup things like collect papers and things. And Grandma walked on the beach to collect shells with them.

Their parents never came here, preferring the pool at the club. There were no waiters or bathrooms, or whatever it was that mommy wanted.

It was harder to get here after their grandparents died. But Grandpa and Grandma had left the Sea Turtle Resort to the Gulfside Girls. Their granddaughters. So, technically, they owned it. But Daddy did the grownup things. "I'll hold it for you two.

Consider it a dowry." Belinda suspected Daddy liked the place too, but Mommy was in charge.

They loved spending the day at the beach! Boy watching, dolphin spotting, and collecting shells were their chief occupations. Every time they collected shells now, they thought of Grandma.

Mommy hated the shells.

"They smell," was her complaint. Belinda knew that anything associated with the cottages was tacky to Mommy. But luckily, Mommy had other worries. Like shopping and socializing and decorating and making Daddy dress a certain way.

Now that Belinda could drive, they were back in business! Her driver's license was brand new. She'd just got it in the mail. Starting in February, she'd been driving them out here whenever they wanted! Joetta had her learner's permit. Next year, they'd take turns behind the wheel.

And Daddy might not have wanted them to drive his car, but he also didn't say no. That was Mommy's job. Today, they took Daddy's keys and drove with the top down.

Erline, their family's maid, packed them peanut butter sandwiches in wax paper, pickles, and even peaches, so they wouldn't "starve," she said, sweetly. Though Belinda was worried about dieting lately, thanks to Mommy. Well, if she swam all day, she'd burn off the sandwiches, hopefully.

Joetta handed Belinda a mangled tube of white paste, zinc oxide. Belinda put it on her nose, which was now pealing for the fiftieth time this summer.

"The smell, why does it have to smell like that?" Joetta scrunched up her little button nose that was freckled from similar scorching.

"Why can't my legs get color instead of my nose every time?" Belinda was trying to achieve an even tan, but of course, it was her nose and shoulders that got it. Her thighs, ugh, they were still light, a tiny bit of color at best. She wanted them savage!

Yes, as the Gulfside Girls lay on their straw mats, the main consideration and worry in their lives was getting that even tan.

"Flip, the back of your legs are dark, and the front isn't," Joetta, the baby sister, advised Belinda.

"Well, if he doesn't get here soon, Mommy is going to flip because we told her we'd be at the club in time for dinner."

"Oh, please, he's going to be here. I know it."

And Belinda knew it, too. Joetta was the prettiest girl on the beach, and she was always attracting admirers. Normally, Joetta was the one in charge of the situation. She dangled her affections in front of the local boys like a carrot. It was sort of sad. But then again, if they were stupid enough to think they were "the one and only," they were stupid.

This new boy was different, though. Joetta was not in charge. He was. He was tall, broad-shouldered, and more muscular than the country club set they normally mingled with.

And older. Belinda didn't know exactly how old, but he wasn't a teen like them.

And honestly, he was a little scary in that he didn't really talk much. He probably had seen too many Steve McQueen movies or something.

They waited and worked on getting every square inch of their bodies as brown as possible.

Suddenly, Joetta said to Belinda, "I'm going to tell you a secret. You cannot tell. Anyone. Even Christie Lee."

They called Christie Lee "Middle Sister," even though Christie Lee wasn't their sister. They'd essentially added her as a mutual best friend. The two sets of parents had deemed their friendship acceptable socially. That was a relief. It was how they all got away with being away. "We're going to Middle Sister's!" they'd say. Or Christie Lee would say she was sleeping over at Belinda and Joetta's. Their parents never checked. It was how the Gulfside Girls could be essentially free and feral and away from the country club expectations of Mommy.

And now Joetta was telling Belinda to keep something from Middle. They weren't in the business of keeping things from Middle, so Belinda knew it really did have to be a huge secret.

"Swear."

The two sisters put their palms together and did a quarter turn. It was their own secret salute.

Joetta took and deep breath then blurted, "I think I'm going to go all the way."

Belinda didn't react. She wanted to gasp, wanted to warn her not to! To be careful! More than that, though, not to do anything before Belinda got a chance to.

She knew, as the older sister, that she was supposed to provide the guidance on these things. But she had nothing to share. No words of wisdom on "all the way." Even though Belinda was only a year older, she should be more worldly. Except, their world was mostly this tiny town, this beach.

So, she sat there quietly, wondering what the right thing was to say. She did not want to act like their mom—square, stuffy, scandalized by everything they did.

Even though the worst thing they did was wear patched skirts they got at the swap meet instead of the Lilly Pulitzer dresses their mother favored for them. Mommy hated their outfits and thought they should both still be dressing like Jackie Kennedy—White House Jackie, not Jackie O. Mommy was very into labels.

Faced with the news that Joetta planned to go all the way, Belinda stayed quiet. She didn't warn Joetta. She didn't act like a prude.

But in her chest, she felt a little fear. Things were more out of control with this new boy than she realized.

"Why him?" she asked.

"He's just so much more exciting than Banks and that crowd. He's a veteran. He has that tattoo, and he does what he wants. He has a job already. He makes cars!"

"Wow, I didn't know that. Yeah, he's no Banks Armstrong, for sure. *His* biggest worry is borrowing his father's Lincoln and hoping no one smokes in it. But, you know, he'd do anything for you." Belinda liked Banks; she understood him. And honestly, the way Joetta ignored him broke her heart.

"He's nice, I guess," Joetta conceded. "But boring."

Joetta had a wild streak that drove their parents crazy, but secretly, it scared Belinda, too.

"And his threads, so real, you know?"

"Yes. I know."

No madras plaid or huarache sandals for this strong and silent out-of-town boy. He really wasn't a boy at all. That's the warning Belinda knew she should give Joetta. That's what she should say. That she should keep the training wheels on with someone like Banks a bit longer before she went all the way with this new guy. He wasn't even from here.

But she didn't say that either.

She also worried that Joetta was drinking full-strength beer with that boy from out of town. Joetta was not good at drinking beer yet. They'd get good at it. In fact, that was one of Belinda's goals for the summer, learning to look cool drinking beer. But right now, they had no idea how to look cool drinking beer—and, blech, the taste!

Plus, it was only a matter of time before their parents smelled the beer on Joetta.

"Well, he better get here soon," Belinda said finally. "I'm not going to want to hear Mommy hassle us and not let us come out tomorrow."

"Right on!"

Joetta's gaze moved from the water to a spot on the beach where a broad-shouldered man with cut-offs, aviator sunglasses, and the look of someone who'd been somewhere other than here walked up and stood at the end of their mat. He was striking-looking. His jaw was square. He did look a little like Clint Eastwood, if

Belinda was being honest. But he wasn't a boy. And he shouldn't be played with.

"Hey," he said. That was it.

Hey. Man of few words, every time.

"Cover for me," Joetta told Belinda. "Tell Mom, I'm uh, at Middle's. Okay?"

As Joetta said it, she grabbed her beach bag, put her t-shirt and shorts in it, and took the man's hand.

Joetta was out to lunch on this. But then again, she was out to lunch on most things.

Belinda watched as Joetta's small hand disappeared into the hand of the strong and silent man from out of town.

Well, no one will bother Joetta with this bruiser on her arm, that's for sure.

Belinda watched them walk away. Just then, Banks Armstrong plopped down next to her beach mat. She turned and could tell from his expression that he had also been watching the scene.

"She's going out with him again?"

"Yes, crushing on him these days."

"I don't see it."

Belinda noticed a pulse in Bank's jaw. He was handsome, too, but Belinda saw the difference. She understood. Banks was what their parents would pick, and Bruce was who you picked to make your parents flip.

Poor Banks. He tried to be cool all the time, but she knew he'd give anything to date Joetta. But Joetta had made her pick.

Well, for today, anyway.

Fourteen

ALI – Present Day

Didi was a lovely hostess. That much was clear.

But she was also too old or too frail to be doing all she was trying to do. That was also clear.

When her husband Jorge made his way into the office with a walker, Ali started to get a sense of just why this place didn't have a working phone, a clean beach towel, or a single guest.

Jorge was more salt than pepper in his wavy hair. He was tanner than Didi but had the same welcoming smile. Didi popped up from her chair and scurried around to be sure Jorge was safely sorted out. They were all situated around a card table in a tiny space that also had a sink and a fridge. It was more makeshift break room than a kitchen. It sat behind a door. On the other side of the door was the counter where guests checked in and did laundry.

"I do apologize for the state of things," Jorge said. "She won't let me do my job and can't do it herself. Stubborn, that's what it's called."

Jorge was a doll, straight up, Ali decided.

"You should know," Didi countered.

Well, they were both too cute for words. Ali felt a little twinge. This was what a lifelong love looked like.

"This looks like a lot of work for anyone, much less someone with a new hip," Ali pointed out.

Didi sighed. "I used to do all the laundry, all of it, same day, honestly. I'll get caught up."

Ali spied the little kitchen sink and fridge in the office.

"Here, you two sit, and I'm guessing this is where your famous lemonade is?" Ali got up, deciding to take over a bit. These two needed help, not to serve her, the woman who'd turned their world upside down out of the blue.

"It is. But you shouldn't be the one serving us! You're the guest," Didi insisted again.

"Well, if my Toledo lawyer is right, I'm actually not. I'm the owner. As such, I'm pouring the drinks."

Jorge and Didi were on edge, and Ali felt bad about that. But no matter how much Didi insisted on working, Ali could see sitting was a good idea for this pair, at least for now.

As Didi popped back up and got the glasses, Jorge put his hand out to help steady his wife. She slid a hand across his shoulder as she passed. These little tokens of love and affection both warmed Ali and made her sad.

She hadn't really mourned the death of her marriage, only the death of her father. But sitting with these two sweet people made her sad that she'd never have that with Ted.

She brushed off the melancholy and refocused on her purpose in Haven Beach.

"How long have you two been managing here?"

"Oh, not long, fifteen years?" Didi asked Jorge, who nodded in confirmation.

"I used to manage facilities for a three-building resort in St. Pete," Jorge explained. "This place is tiny comparatively, so perfect for my retirement."

"Ha, retired," Didi laughed. "We work every day! That's the key to our vitality. Which we had, until six months ago, his hip, my heart. It's like pffft. Bam! You're old!" Didi snapped her fingers.

Didi didn't say this was sadness. She smiled and laughed at their current state.

Her positive energy was contagious. Ali found herself enjoying their company and this space.

"I had been retired for a few years," Didi continued. "It was so boring! I really needed a change of pace, so we signed on here. We live across the street. It's a really nice condo. We used to live on the property, but the condo has space when the grandkids come. We're always booked here, or, uh, we used to be before my mess up with the phone. And the pool. Oh, dear. You're visiting at a terrible time. I'm so embarrassed."

"No judgment. I literally just found out about this whole thing. Curious, why don't you have online booking or a service like VRBO?"

"Ah, no. I suppose we're old-fashioned that way. But if you are the new boss, you can get all that new-fangled stuff!"

"I don't know about being the new boss. I inherited this from, uh. Well. I don't have the details. But I do need to assess the financial realities here. And I need to understand before we put it on the market."

Didi gasped and then put her hand up to her mouth. But the woman's brain was working, that much was clear. She adjusted and pitched, "Of course, I mean, you're smart to do that. But what about keeping it as an investment or as your family's summer place?"

Ali had no intention of that. "I'm not the sole owner," she told them. "All three of us, my sisters that is, are listed for the property. I'm the oldest and just recently quit my job, so I had time to come down and check things out."

"And you just found the paperwork?"

"Yes, my father died, and it was amongst some things of his. I still don't know why he never told us about it. I'm wondering about the management company. I'll need to speak with them. Do you have some contact info I can get my hands on?"

"Oh, sure, uh, Jorge, is that in our files at home? That contact info?"

"Huh?"

"You know, the management company information?" Didi squeezed Jorge on the shoulder and gave him a wife-to-husband stare. Ali had no idea what Jorge had done wrong, but he was for sure getting the stink eye from Didi all of a sudden.

He looked from his wife to Ali and then said, "Yes, uh, corporate stuff, hard to remember the name, always changing."

"Well, if you could get that."

"It'll have to be tomorrow; we've got quite a bit of work to finish here, and we both have doctor's appointments and then the meeting."

"Sure, I've interrupted your day, and I can see there's a lot to do here. If you don't mind, I'll just come back by tomorrow."

"Where are you staying? Can I drive you back?" Jorge offered.

"No, my car is here. I can head back on my own. I'm over at the Courtyard Marriott."

"Blech! No, no, no!" Didi waved her hands in the air.

"What?"

"You should stay *here*. To really understand the Sea Turtle, you need to spend a night in a cottage."

"What about your guests?" As Ali said it, she realized she hadn't seen a single one.

"The Key Lime Cottage is closest to the water. It's adorable. Get your bag from the hotel, check out, and just move in here! It's perfect!"

Didi had it all settled for Ali.

"I don't want to be an imposition."

"Please, you're the boss, not us. And if you really want to

93

know what you've got here, you have to live here, for a day and night at least."

"Live here?"

"Oh, figure of speech, but you could explore our grounds all day. Take a dip in the water, walk on the beach, and a few of our neighbors might even swing by for the Grand Finale."

By this point Ali knew what that was, the sunset. She'd missed it last night.

"I don't know."

Didi reached out and took Ali's hands in hers. Ali was taken aback. There was something so touching about it. This woman, old enough to be her mother but younger in spirit than Ali herself, locked eyes with her.

"You need what this beach has. I feel it. Sand between your toes, ocean breeze, and those waves lulling you to sleep. I promise you'll soak it in and go back to Ohio as good as new. I'll even make us some snacks."

"She makes good snacks, I'll give her that," Jorge chimed in. "Can't dance at all, but man, the cheese board." Jorge gave Ali a wink.

Something caught in Ali's throat. Emotion? Recognition? Or was it just having these two kind people be sweet to her? She'd hate to disrupt their lives by selling this place, which she was going to have to do.

But it did make sense, staying one night, getting the lay of the land. And she had to admit, the place had a funky charm. The Marriott was nice, but it looked like every other hotel she'd ever been in. She could have been back home in Toledo when she closed the door. Here, well, here you were on the beach, no question.

"Okay, I'll stay the day and night."

Didi smiled, and it took over her whole face. She was ageless when she smiled.

And then, a question popped into Ali's mind.

"How did you know I was from Ohio?"

Didi's smile flickered, and she waved her hand in the air.

"Your accent, total Ohio accent. We get a lot of snowbirds."

Ali nodded and then stood up. "Okay, well, I'll go get my bag and check out. See you in an hour!"

She was feeling lighter than she'd felt in weeks.

Maybe I do need what this beach has, even if just for one night.

Fifteen

FAYE

"These grades are terrible. You're smart. This is just laziness!"

Sawyer was flunking out of college. There was no way to sugarcoat it.

He grunted in response to her observation. "I'm in a bunch of classes I have no interest in."

"You're in them? Or do you not go to them?"

Faye suspected her son was sleeping during the day and enjoying the social aspect of college but not the college aspect of college.

Faye was footing the bill for The Ohio State University. And it was a lot of money to be spending on Ds and Fs.

While Ali's two kids had free tuition thanks to their dad, Professor Ted, Faye had no such luck in the baby daddy department. Faye and Sawyer had been on their own since she'd kicked Buddy, her ex, out. No child support or college savings had come her way from Buddy.

She didn't know what Sawyer remembered. He was only five

years old when Faye gave Buddy the boot. Sawyer was the better of two souvenirs Faye had from Buddy. The worst souvenir was a scar that interrupted her left eyebrow, a remnant from the stitches she'd needed when Buddy had pushed her into the door frame. She put her finger up to that spot and rubbed it, as she knew she did when she was stressed out.

Did Sawyer remember seeing me stagger back up? Did he remember me scooping him up and driving over to my sister's?

He probably didn't remember much. Faye had been divorced now more than twice as long as she'd been married.

Buddy was a boozer. She was, too, at the time. It was the only way to spend time with him. But when she became a mom, she'd lost interest in going out. She'd become less into partying and more into *Barney the Dinosaur*. The more Buddy drank, the meaner he got, until that night he split her forehead.

Buddy was a good-looking, too-cool-for-school loser. He was such a loser that he'd spent very little time trying to connect with Sawyer, their son. A son who looked just like his dad. And, right now, the aimless party attitude had Faye fearing they were alike in more ways than looks.

Faye had always made good money at the plant. She'd raised Sawyer on her own. He was a great athlete but not college scholarship level. Still, he'd gotten into the OSU with good test scores. She thought she'd succeeded, that there was a magical finish line she'd crossed when she got him to college.

But he was failing now. Big time. And Faye didn't know what to do.

"I don't want to be there."

"What? It's a great school. There are so many options and opportunities!"

"I just, well...I don't know what I want, but it's not that."

Faye's heart sank. *Now what?* She'd aimed this kid for college and now that he seemed aimless, she didn't know the next course to take. He was eighteen, almost nineteen, but also sometimes still such a baby. He was veering off course, and that finish line was nowhere in sight. When he was in high school, she could check that his assignments were in, she could meet with teachers when he was slacking, and she could remind him about tests. But in college, none of that was available to a parent. And she got it. She didn't want to helicopter his every move.

What can I do? What does my baby man-boy need to get him closer to adulthood?

Faye improvised a temporary fix to the current dilemma until she could really help Sawyer sort out his future.

"How about this? You finish this semester. But you give it your all. I mean, no more skipping class."

"I'm not skip—"

"—Sawyer, you're smart. You know it, and I know it. The only way you're pulling a 2.0 in World History is by skipping World History. Your only good grade is glass blowing. Glass blowing?"

"Mom, I'm making a planter, like a terrarium, really, for the fern you started?"

Sawyer had been by her side when she planted her garden out back. Her assistant. And when he'd grown a foot taller than her, she'd paid him to push wheelbarrows and haul mulch.

Faye sighed. "I think you're selling yourself short, but I hear you. You're not happy there. Can we make this deal? You give it your all, like I said, finish out the year as best you can. And we put this on the table in the spring. I'll listen to the things you're thinking about doing, and you'll, well, you'll just try."

Sawyer shifted on his feet; his blond shank of hair flopped over his eye.

She reached over and brushed it away.

"Okay. Deal. But this spring, no big drama if I want to drop out."

"No big drama. But you need to try."

"Fine. Fine."

Her phone buzzed. It was work. She picked it up. "Yeah, no. Yeah." She hung up.

"You have to go in?"

"Mandatory overtime, yes, I do."

Her son rolled his eyes. He knew if work called, Faye would answer. She never felt guilty about that. It was how he had nice clothes, that skateboard, and that game system. But right now, she wished she could sit with him a little longer, maybe order a pizza together.

But work called. And she answered.

She was about to put her phone in her bag, when it vibrated. A text from Ali. A picture of the cutest little lime green house popped up on her phone. *What the heck?*

She read the text:

Staying here tonight. We own it, lol. Wish me luck. The roof leaks and the mosquitos are as big as chihuahuas.

She sent a thumbs-up emoji and went to the plant. *Well, at least it wasn't snowing*, Faye thought as she drove.

Sixteen

ALI

It didn't take long for Ali to have her Jeep packed again. She was ready to make her home for a day at the Sea Turtle Resort.

Didi greeted her and directed her to park her Jeep around a little corner. "This way, the palm trees will shade your car a bit! And our guests can park."

Ali smiled and wondered what the older woman meant by guests, as she still hadn't seen any.

"Oh, yeah, the cottages are empty, but I do have three at the Inn." Didi pointed to the structure next to the pool.

The pool looked gross to Ali. A sign with a turtle and a cartoon bubble announced that it was closed.

Thank goodness, Ali thought. It did not look safe.

"Jorge needs to call our guy, Silvio," Didi told her. "He's been so stubborn about doing it all himself." She added that Jorge was taking a little nap. "You know he had a hip replacement, which is not supposed to take this long to recover from, but then there was a problem with the oil in the joint of the thing they put in. Anyway, THAT had to be fixed, and he battled an infection. I was really scared there for a bit. But anyway, that was at the end of the season last year. We thought he'd be ready to go for this season, but well, he's not quite back to normal yet."

Ali knew what it was like to deal with an aging man, one used to doing it all on his own. "Ha, I get it, my dad was like that the last few years. Not that it's the last few years for your husband, but I'll tell you, it's hard to get a man like that to release control of the things they're used to doing."

"Amen, you understand!"

Ali smiled at Didi. "So, can you give me the lay of the land, if that's okay?"

"Yes, yes, do you want to go to the hotel first?"

"Okay."

They walked the path around the pool and into the hotel section of the Sea Turtle. There was a charm to the building, and at only two stories, it was tiny compared to what she'd seen up and down the Gulf.

"Only six rooms?"

"And the penthouse."

"Gotcha."

An open-air walkway connected the rooms, each of which appeared to have its own little balcony.

"We struggle sometimes because the big places have kitchens and laundry inside, and on and on. Our units have a bedroom, a mini fridge, and a bathroom. We've got doubles and singles, so a family could stay, but, well. Maybe bigger is better for some?"

"Bigger is more expensive," Ali commented. Maybe that was the problem. They couldn't charge much if they didn't offer much.

"Here, this room is a good example of Sea Turtle Inn's offerings."

Didi used an old-fashioned key and opened the door to the

room. It was odd, these days, to check in and have a key instead of a card. Ali hadn't seen a hotel room key in years, she realized.

The room was warm, too warm.

"Oh darn it all." Didi walked over to the wall where an ancient-looking air conditioner sat quietly.

Didi clicked the knob on and off and on. Then she hit the side with a surprisingly strong whack. The unit responded with a humming noise and a squeak that sounded as if the thing was powered by a hamster running on a wheel inside the panel.

"Why don't I open the window?" Ali walked to the end of the room and opened the drapes, which were yellowed and out of style by at least fifteen years.

She pushed them open, and the gorgeous view took her breath away.

"Wow, just wow."

The sun was high; the sky, pure blue, with not a cloud in sight. And the beach stretched out as far as she could see. There was a little balcony, enough for maybe two chairs and a coffee table, but there was nothing on it at the moment.

Ali stepped out and took the view in.

"It's the money shot! All of the rooms have this view, which makes us unique. For some reason Jorge says I should not call it the money shot, something inappropriate. Anyway, it *is* the money shot." Didi laughed at herself, and Ali couldn't help chuckling, too.

"You're not wrong, it's impressive."

It was hard to believe that the place wasn't completely booked all the time when you took into consideration that all six rooms were ocean view.

Ali scanned the outside of the building from this new angle. Was the roof in need of repair? She saw some water damage on the exterior of the building. She bounced a little on the balcony, all of a sudden wondering if the thing was safe. It didn't give, not even a tiny bit. That made her feel a little better. There were things in disrepair, neglect even, but Jorge's long convalescence explained a lot of it.

"I'm sure we could use some sprucing up." Didi looked a little sheepish, but Ali felt an impulse to defend her. To bolster her.

"Nonsense, this place is charming! You're doing a wonderful job."

Ali had realized that now, technically, she was the boss. She didn't want the elderly couple to feel bad about their work. Especially seeing as they'd had some challenges lately.

Didi smiled back at her and reached out to squeeze her hand. "You're a glass half full gal, I like that. Me too."

They finished the tour, and Ali saw the appeal, over and over, of the little hotel. But she also could hear someone like Ted complaining about modern amenities, as he often did when they took family vacations.

"Now, I love the hotel section, don't get me wrong," Didi gushed, "but the Sea Turtle Beach Cottages? Oh, they're my favorite."

Didi continued to list the attributes of the Sea Turtle Resort, and Ali listened. She peppered the older woman with a question now and then, but mostly, she let Didi regale her with stories.

"There's a story that Frank Sinatra stayed in the penthouse once. And someone has a picture of it. But, of course, that's just a fun story."

"Wow. Okay." Ali could almost see the place back in the '50s or '60s. Too bad it was shellacked over with the '80s. The rooms were simple but all you needed. The vacation was outside, not in.

Didi continued. "One year, when Hurricane Hamish came through, this was a little lake. But don't worry, we, guests included, baled and baled, and within the week, we were back in business! That's the thing, people who stay here come back. It's their oasis away from home. Or, well, it was."

Ali felt sad for the older woman; she loved this place, and the glory days it had were clearly in the rearview.

The resort property was half the hotel and half this almost village or cul-de-sac of cottages. They walked there now. The six little shacks were arranged so that each had direct beach view and access, though two were clearly the "best" and seemed just plopped down on the sandy shore.

A little courtyard featured a fire pit and palm trees. There was a grill, a shuffleboard court, and quirky faded cartoon turtles at different points instructing guests which way to the laundry or beach or hotel.

"We used to have a play area, the Hatchling Hutch. It had a swing set. But that was a while ago." Didi waved over to the side, next to the roped-off pool. "All in all, Sea Turtle Resort is two acres along the beach and half an acre deep! Big, really, despite how cozy we are."

Ali's jaw dropped again. *Over two acres? On the Gulf of Mexico?* It hadn't really dawned on her before how much that really was.

Ali was no real estate expert, but she knew that this wasn't what people rented these days for vacation. They wanted cartoon characters and superheroes and WiFi and continental breakfasts.

But resale...this had to be worth something. The acreage alone. Was this life-changing money for her and her sisters if they could unload it?

Of course, Ali didn't mention unloading it to Didi. Tough conversations were ahead, and she'd had too many tough conversations in her recent past. She just enjoyed the tour, and the stories lovingly conveyed by a native Floridian. Ali wasn't sure if she'd ever met someone *from* Florida, only people who'd moved *to* Florida.

The six cottages were in various states, from dilapidated to almost good. Each was a different color of peeling paint. There was the Lemon Love Shack, the Strawberry Hideaway, the Pink Lady, the Blueberry Bungalow, the Mango Mansion, and the Key Lime.

After a walking tour of the cottage section, Didi and Ali arrived at the lime green clapboard structure. It had a weathered porch and a faded wooden sign to indicate that this was the Key Lime Cottage—in case the lime paint hadn't already given it away.

Each cottage had a wooden deck, and each deck was in some level of distress. Ali wondered when the last time major repairs or restorations had happened. She really needed to see the books and find out. The Key Lime looked to be the freshest of the cottages. The wood deck was newer, and the deck rail was straight, with all the slats intact. The decks were small, but Ali noted they could accommodate a couple of chairs and maybe a little bistro table.

She had to stop. She wasn't here to decorate. She was here to unload!

"Here, this is your cottage, the Key Lime. I've stocked you with some water in the kitchen and fresh towels, sheets, all that!"

They walked in and the word cute wasn't big enough to describe what Ali saw. The entry door was to the side, and two large windows faced out to the ocean view.

Ali stepped into the space and did a 360-degree turn. A couch, two comfy chairs, and a kitchen table for four made it cozy but not cluttered. The small kitchen appeared to have all one would need, from a stove, oven, fridge, and sink. In the center of the far wall, a hallway split with a bathroom and a bedroom beyond the doors.

"You're smiling. You sure have a gorgeous smile, young lady!"

Ali hadn't realized she'd busted into a smile. It had just happened when she'd stepped into the Key Lime.

"I'm, uh, thank you. Haven't had a lot of reasons to smile lately."

"Well, the Key Lime has that effect on me too."

Ali realized, though, that this big stupid smile wasn't getting her mission accomplished, her mission of finding out the management company contact information, of getting this place appraised, of finding a reputable commercial real estate agent. She wasn't down here for vacation! Yet, the sound of the ocean, the salty fresh air in this little space, and the sweet older couple who welcomed her had distracted her from the job at hand. The job she came to do.

"Did you have a chance to get that contact information, the management firm?"

"Oh, goodness, we've been so busy. I haven't yet, and we've got the Grand Finale yet. I'll put it on your tray for breakfast. Does that work?"

Ali didn't want to put Didi out any more than she had. There was clearly a lot on the woman's plate, and she'd been kind and patient as they toured the grounds.

"Sure, sure, of course."

"Now, I need you to get into your way more casual beach togs, dip your toes in the ocean, nap, whatever you need. And a little after six, join us for the Grand Finale."

"I don't really have, uh, beach togs."

"I figured as much. There are a few things in the closet. I had them brought over—they're from when I was more your size, than mine. If you don't mind vintage, they will work."

"Oh, you didn't need to do that. You're very sweet."

"See you at the Grand Finale. We'll be out there with a glass of wine and a lounge with your name on it."

Didi left Ali on her own in the Key Lime.

She decided Didi's advice was best followed. Something made the woman happy, peaceful, and easy to be around.

Maybe it was the kaftan!

She walked over a distressed wood floor, trying not to imagine refinishing them, and to the bedroom closet. She found several brightly colored flowy gowns neatly hung in a row.

"Wow! Mrs. Roper should be so lucky."

She reached out at touched the fabric. She decided the coral with blue and teal looked about right. Ali got rid of her khaki pants, too-stiff white blouse, and loafers. She put on her bathing suit first and then reached for the kaftan.

She read the label: *Emilio Pucci.*

It gave her an idea. Maybe Didi would be able to help her value their late mother's garments. She clearly also had an eye for designers, though looking at her today, she was all about the t-shirt and shorts.

Ali slipped into the kaftan, and another bit of the Midwest winter back home fluttered away.

She was starting to see what lured the migration of the snowbirds. Ali had time for a little rest before Didi and Jorge expected her outside.

Ali added Haven Beach to her weather app and then scanned the seven-day forecast:

Sunny, warm, sunny, warm, sunny, warm, sunny.

Seventeen

ALI

Ali napped. What was with her? She *never* napped. But the salt air, the breeze, and the sound of the ocean right outside the little Key Lime Cottage had her more relaxed than she'd been in...she didn't know how long. Had she ever been this relaxed?

It was past dinner when she woke up. She looked at her phone and slid the weather app to the weather in Toledo. *Gray, slushy, blech.* Everyone loved the fluffy snow in December, but January into February? Not so much. She'd made a career of convincing convention selection committees that Frogtown Convention Center would be lovely all year round. And it was, but she did have to offer good discounts in the winter to get the thing booked. Selling the Midwest in December was easy. In February or March? A bit of a slog.

Well, that wasn't her challenge anymore. Let Jerry figure out how to book next winter. Or manage the custodial staff, who she knew, was getting very frustrated with the budget cuts Jerry wanted to make.

Not your problem Ali Kelly, not your problem.

Her problem was getting a divorce from Ted. She hadn't let that be at the top of her mind since her marriage imploded the same day her father died. She'd used the endless tasks of the end of his life to avoid the end of her marriage. Ali supposed she should think about it all, though. Unpack what went wrong. But it all made her so sad, defeated. She decided to avoid that Pandora's Box for now. Plus, there were no messages from Barb Burns, her divorce attorney, so she would just trust things on that depressing front were moving as they should.

She did miss the kids though; she always missed the kids. Even when she was in Toledo.

Maybe that was a condition of having adult kids and no grand-kids? She'd have to get used to that, she supposed.

She had a group text with Katie and Tye, so she texted a few pictures of the Key Lime and the ocean.

No response from either. Which was typical. If they texted her, she responded like there was a fire. If she texted them, now that they were in college, she'd get a response a day or so later.

While they were in high school, there was a strict proof of life policy, a "you-have-one-minute-to-respond" situation for texting. But now that they were out in the world—well, over on Bancroft Street at the University—she didn't make rules like that anymore. Though she did still pay for the cell phones.

She and Ted did, that was. There was going to be a fair amount to untangle. She couldn't untangle it tonight, and she was getting a little hungry. Ali decided it was time to see this Grand Finale she'd heard about from the proprietor of the Seashell Shack and Didi.

She slid on her lone pair of flip-flops. And she really had to appreciate how getting in the right wardrobe got her in a more relaxed mindset. This vintage kaftan was light, cool, and, best of all, no binding anywhere. She didn't feel compelled to suck anything in. She was so tired of sucking things in.

For a moment, she worried that she didn't have something to

bring to Didi and Jorge. Was that rude? Was this a social event? She had no idea.

Ali shrugged and went out the front door of Key Lime. At the end of the path that ran in the center of the little village of cottages, there was the gorgeous beach. She spied Jorge sitting in a lounge that looked quite comfortable. She saw Didi pouring wine for a lanky figure of a man. As she got closer, she realized it was the owner of the Seashell Shack. Apparently, Haven Beach was a small world.

Ali started toward them, but then sand weighed down her flip-flops. They were not necessary; the hot sand had cooled as the sun sank. She kicked them both off and hooked them on her left finger.

The sinking sun. That was the show, she now fully understood.

The sun looked like an over-ripe orange. The sky was a light blue tinged with pink. The horizon was a different blue and tinged with the orange.

She stood in place and stared. As she did, the sun sank further toward the waterline.

"Ali! Get over here, I've got a glass ready for you." Didi had a bottle of wine and a full glass of white wine. She handed it over, and Ali thanked her.

"We've got a tray of cheese and snacks over by Jorge. This is Henry Hawkins. He owns a restaurant about three units over. You have to have his crab cakes."

"I have had them, delicious."

"You're looking like local now, much better." Henry complimented her on her kaftan.

"Ha, well, courtesy of Didi."

He sure was handsome, and casual, and cool. Ali realized she was having high school-type thoughts. *Get over it. This is not* MTV *Spring Break, you old lady!*

"We're similarly vertically challenged," Didi chuckled.

"It looks lovely on both of you," Henry said.

"And here," Didi told Ali, "this is Erica Bell. She runs Morning Bell, the best coffee on the beach. It's a must."

"Hello! Welcome! Hey, Didi?" Erica pointed to her wine glass.

The woman's boho vibe was something Ali aspired to have without knowing it. Cut-off shorts, dozens of bracelets, a colorful smock, and wild steel dreads topped off the look.

"Yes, yes! My apologies." Didi filled Erica's glass.

"I'm off tomorrow, my daughter is taking the whole day for me, so I can go crazy!"

"Crazy for Erica is two glasses," Henry said to Ali.

"Okay," Didi said, business-like once more. "We have a few hotel guests. I'm going to go make sure they're enjoying the Grand Finale. If they can't use the pool, at least they'll be glad they got some free vino!"

"Good plan," Erica said. "Here, sit, chill." She guided all three of them to two chairs and a nearby beach blanket.

"You ladies take the chairs, I'm good on the sand." Henry plopped down on the beach blanket, and Ali heard a distinct pop.

"Are you okay?" she asked, concerned he'd hurt himself.

"Ah, yes, my knees love making that sound these days."

"Oh, you know it, mine too," Erica replied. "And I didn't even play baseball like this one. I was getting on the ladder, and it was like pop rocks." The two laughed.

Ali could relate. Lately, getting down on the floor was easy, but getting up, well, that was another story.

"What do you do, Ali?" Henry asked.

"I am the assistant to the manager and event coordinator of Frogtown Convention Center. Uh, well, I was, until a couple of weeks ago."

"Whoa, that sounds like a lot of work," Erica said.

"It was. I liked it, though, mostly."

"Frogtown, I forgot that nickname," Henry said.

"Ah, yes, we also have the Black Swamp, The Glass City, all Toledo."

"You were in Toledo, right?" Jorge asked Henry. "For a season?"

"Yep, in my downward baseball career, that was a stop," Henry said and took a sip of the wine. He said it with good humor.

"We get a lot of Toledo and Detroit folks around here in about a month or so," Erica told Ali. "Spring break. Every once in a while, a baseball fanatic recognizes him."

"They have to be a really committed fanatic," Henry said modestly.

"Stop, you're locally famous, anyway."

"For my crab cakes!"

"They *were* delicious," Ali chimed in and then turned her focus back to the horizon. The sun appeared to bob on the top of the water now. "It's fast, this sunset thing."

"You know it," Erica agreed. "Just yesterday, I was in a wet t-shirt contest hosted by Ken Ober, and now I'm wondering if I should increase the dose of my estrogen patch."

Henry and Erica laughed, and Ali felt included immediately. Like these old friends were opening their circle to her with no hesitation. What sweet people she'd met in the last two days. It was as if some of the normal stressors of life were in better proportion here than back home.

Ali created a stack of cheese and crackers from the selection on the little tray Didi had offered. They were hitting the spot.

"Where are you two from?" she asked Erica and Henry.

"I'm from Chicago, originally, and Henry's from South Carolina," Erica said.

"Everyone's a transplant here, by the way, except Didi and Jorge, they're lifers," Henry added.

"Oh, look!" Erica pointed to the horizon where a fin and then another fin slid up and down on the surface.

"What?" Ali was thinking *Jaws*, but Henry set her right.

"Dolphin family."

"Ah."

The sun sank further now, and almost as if there was an unspoken mutual agreement, every one of the dozen or so people gathered for the Grand Finale stopped chatting. Even Didi stopped flitting from person to person. And they all watched, in quiet, as the sun melted into the water.

The orange orb lit the line of water, seemingly on fire.

Down. Down.

And then there was just a little bump of a flame.

And then gone!

The group erupted in cheers.

"Bravo!"

"Good one!"

"Well done!"

"What do you think, Ali. Worth staying over?" Didi asked, appearing by Ali's side.

"Worth it? Yes, more than worth it. Stunning."

"Yep, another show tomorrow evening. But just so you know, it's never the same show twice," Henry said and lifted a glass to the horizon as if to toast it.

"Okay, see you all tomorrow," Erica called, already making her way back across the sand. "Come over to the coffee shop, Ali. I'll let them know your first cup's on me."

"Oh, thank you, no need to."

"Pshaw. That's how I hook you," Erica grinned.

"Dang, she's good," Henry said. "I should have done the same with the crab cakes. Wait, Jorge, sit down, what the heck?"

Henry popped up off the beach blanket and ran—pretty deftly, in Ali's opinion—over to Jorge, who was struggling to help collect beach chairs.

"No, no. I'm doing this." Henry folded chairs and grabbed the cooler that Didi had brought down from the Sea Turtle.

"Fine, fine, but I'm better. I'm way better," Jorge said.

"I realize that, but my mother would turn over in her grave if her baby boy didn't help pick up after your lovely hospitality."

Henry and Jorge continued to banter as Didi approached Ali again.

"Now you see, a little piece of paradise, right?"

"It appears to be the case. Yes."

"Everyone who stays is invited down here to enjoy the Grand Finale. It's been dwindling, thanks to the issues we're working on, but sometimes we have over two dozen. It's my favorite part of the day. I love that locals like us and our sweet guests mingle and just kick back and appreciate the view."

"And how fast it goes," Ali said again.

Why was that sticking with me?

"Yes, and how fast it all goes."

Didi was talking about life. That was clear. Ali realized she was, too. The sunset made it plain. Time was moving faster than she appreciated.

Ali wanted to ask Didi all the business things she needed to know. But she didn't. Life was speeding by, and she ought to give herself one night of relaxation on the beach. No lists or tasks to accomplish.

Oddly, she felt a little sad. Ali wanted to see what the sun did tomorrow.

Maybe I'll stay a few more days to sort things out.

Eighteen

BELINDA
1974

She'd never seen her mother so angry or her father so cold. Joetta was In Trouble. At sixteen, she'd gotten in the worst trouble they could fathom, and now Belinda sat at the top of the stairs, listening in.

Their mother was yelling, so it was easy to hear.

"I can't show my face anywhere, ANYWHERE, thanks to this. Thanks to *you!*"

Joetta kept trying to get their mother to listen, to help, to understand. "We are going to get married. He loves me."

"That laborer? He's base, and you're too stupid to know it. I raised you to be better than this, and you've thrown it away."

Her little sister was crying, which cut Belinda to the core. She hated to see her sad or even disappointed.

"Daddy. Can you please forgive me? We just need a little to start out."

Their father coughed. And then Belinda heard footsteps. He

was walking away. While their mother berated Joetta, their father walked away. Belinda didn't know which was worse.

"GET OUT OF MY SIGHT!"

Joetta ran now, too. Belinda stood up and was there to catch her little sister as she collapsed into wracking sobs.

This was awful, a mess, the worst mess she could imagine.

"Come on." Belinda led Joetta to her room. She sat her little sister on her bed and found a Kleenex.

"Here, stop. We need you to stop."

"But, but Daddy wouldn't even look at me." The words sputtered out between sobs.

"I know. I know. We have to think. Can you give it up for adoption? Go visit the relatives back east, and then you know, come back here? No one would know."

"No, I won't. I *can't*."

"Why can't you?"

"You're not listening to me either. No one is except him. He listens. He asked me to marry him, and I said yes. Baby or not, I'm marrying him."

"What about Banks? He loves you, I think." Belinda's mind was racing, trying to stop Joetta from marrying this man she hardly knew. Her sister seemed way too young to know what in love really meant.

"What?"

"At least he's here. We know him. He'd do anything for you."

"But I don't love him."

It all began to sink in for Belinda; their lives as sisters, the only lives they'd ever known, were about to change. There was no going back to the two girls on the beach.

In that moment, Belinda grew up, maybe even more than Joetta did, and she was the one In Trouble.

"You need to get out now, then."

"What? I want a wedding. A dress. The club. We can do all that right away, and then no one will even question the rest of it."

"You just said Daddy won't even look at you. He's not going plan a wedding for you."

Joetta swallowed hard. She wiped her eyes. "What do I do?"

Belinda knew, down to her bones, what was next. Mommy and Daddy were going to cut Joetta off. There would be no wedding or registry or any of it. Joetta would be lucky to have whatever was in her piggy bank.

"We start packing. Now."

Belinda grabbed a suitcase from the back of Joetta's closet and laid it on the plush carpet.

Joetta nodded and started adding dresses and shoes and her little pink diary. She put a stuffed animal and a curling iron in the suitcase. Mommy had given them both a set when they went to New York on holiday.

Belinda watched her sister pack for a life that seemed like the one they already lived, where she'd need cocktail dresses, a formal, and her Pucci.

But Belinda doubted the man that had gotten Joetta In Trouble belonged to a country club or went to the Junior League fundraisers with his parents or played shuffleboard. In the few interactions she'd had with him, he barely spoke, much less socialized.

Joetta's life was not going to go like she was fantasizing. She would not be playing house.

That's when Belinda went back to her own room. She opened her piggy bank. She had three hundred dollars in cash. That was a lot. But not enough.

Joetta got the same allowance as Belinda, but she knew her little sister spent it as soon as she got it. She knew Joetta's piggy bank was empty. Next, Belinda went to her jewelry box. She had Grandma Esther's stick pin. Her mother told her never to wear it because the little gold tulip wrapped around a real diamond. She grabbed it.

She also knew Mama had bigger, fancier jewelry. Should she dare?

For a moment, she considered grabbing a fist full of their mother's prized collection but then reconsidered. The way mother and father were behaving, it wouldn't surprise her if they threw Belinda and Joetta in jail if any jewelry came up missing. She thought better of it.

She grabbed the pearls she'd received for her sweet sixteen. That was something. She walked back to Joetta's room to find her sitting on the suitcase trying to close it.

"Here, let me." Belinda sat with her and their combined weight was enough to get it shut.

Belinda walked over to Joetta's matching jewelry box. Her pearls and their Grandma Esther's teardrop earrings were in Joetta's stash.

"Why didn't you pack the jewelry?"

"It's so old-fashioned. I hate it all."

Belinda scooped up the little treasures and added them to the ones she'd brought in.

"What in the world?"

"Here's the cash in my piggy bank. And take my jewelry. I don't know how much it will get you, but it's real, so it has to be worth something."

"He has a job, an apartment, and a car, we don't need to—"

"—Joetta, you don't know what you're getting into. And maybe he does have all the things you'll need, and you love him and all that. Just consider this your shower gift, then. But don't tell him you have it. Just put it in this bag with your makeup. It's for an emergency."

"You're such a good saver."

Joetta did as Belinda instructed. She also took the money and put it in her favorite purse.

"I have to go."

Joetta and Belinda looked into each other's eyes. They'd barely spent a day in their lives apart. And now Joetta was moving away. She was going to have a baby. And she was marrying that man who, if Belinda was being honest, scared her a little. If for no other reason other than that he was so different to them.

Belinda pulled Joetta into her arms. She hugged her hard. "We're always going to be the Gulfside Girls." They put their palms together and did a quarter turn.

Belinda knew that they would likely never be those girls again.

And things were going to change forever.

Nineteen

DIDI

"Jorge. You're not supposed to be doing this."

Didi found her husband with a garden hose and a push broom.

"The pool deck needs hosing off. That's not hard to do."

"No one is using the pool, Jorge, not right now."

Didi tried to grab the broom, but Jorge flicked the water from the garden hose at her.

"Hey!"

He stood his ground. He was a foot taller than she was and surprisingly stronger than he'd been in the last few months.

"I'm serious, Jorge, you don't have approval."

"The doctor said to start doing what I had the energy for. I have the energy to hose some things down. I'd be careful if I were you. You'll be getting an outdoor shower. Though I see you're darn good at dodging. Remarkably good."

Didi put her hands on her hips. "What do you mean?"

"Takes a lot of work to evade a simple question, and you're doing it like it's a sport at the Summer Olympics."

"I don't know what you're talking about."

"Oh, look, serving me up the innocent face. That's one of your cutest faces." Jorge gave her a wink, and she shook it off.

"I'm not serving it up. I am legitimately innocent of whatever it is you're accusing me of."

"I'm just watching you dance around the question that Ali has about who pays us, the name of the management company, and the basics."

"I want to help her."

"I know."

Didi felt defeated, tired, and bowled over by the mere fact that Jorge was right. She was dancing around the question that Ali had every right to ask.

"What's wrong?" Jorge put down the hose and picked up Didi's hands. He guided her to spots on two pool lounges. She helped him sit in one, and she did the same.

He was still handsome, her amazing, strong husband. They'd been through so much and more than they'd bargained for the last six months with his health.

They were seeing the light at the end of the tunnel now though. He was getting stronger. Trying to help clean the pool deck was proof of that.

But now that Ali had showed up, it might all come crashing down.

"What are you worried about?"

"The truth."

"You've never shied away from the truth since I met you."

Jorge knew most of the story. He'd have never retired with her here if he hadn't known exactly how it was going to work. Well, he knew *most* of the story.

"She owns it. There's no two ways about it."

"Ali has her head on straight," Jorge said, trying to reassure her. "I don't think it's a bad thing that she's here."

"No, it's not. I've wanted this. Very much. But now I have to try to unravel it. Try to explain."

"You can do it."

"Not yet, Jorge, not yet."

"What?"

"I'm going to get her to stay. She has to stay."

"What?"

"Oh, nothing. Nothing. Keep working with the hose. I'll stop nagging you. But don't work too hard. Listen to your body."

"What are you up to?"

"Never mind."

"Didi, you have to tell her the truth. She's not going to continue to be put off by this story that you don't know who pays us, for crying out loud!"

"Just hush. And trust me."

"Didi, the truth."

"I will. I will. As soon as I've got her. I had her pretty good last night at the Grand Finale. A little more nudge from the ocean and this place, and we'll have her."

"Retirement isn't a bad word."

Didi paused in her fevered plans and looked at Jorge. He'd never really wanted to retire. He'd never wanted to admit he couldn't do all the things needed here. In the beginning, this place was nothing compared to the big complex that he'd managed. But here they were, celebrating a victory because he had the energy to wash the cement.

They were getting too old for this.

Maybe this was fate. Ali walking into the Sea Turtle Resort when she did was a good thing. In a way, an answer to Didi's prayers.

The next time the younger woman asked about who paid them, she'd show her the books.

There was one bank account they deposited in to and used to maintain the Sea Turtle. They also paid themselves from it. There was no mystery there. It wasn't even complicated.

There also used to be extra, a nest egg Didi had plans for, but now, well, that was dwindling.

Maybe it was best to hold off on opening the books just a bit longer.

Long enough to convince Ali this was her home.

That would require Henry to keep showing up. Ali had an eye for him. Didi could see that! And Erica was Ali's age. Didi would keep pulling Ali into their little Haven Beach community. If Ali was anything like Didi, she would have a hard time leaving it.

Haven Beach was made for second acts and spectacular sunsets. Ali would see it in time.

Ali had no kids with her, no husband, and no wedding ring on. But Didi had noticed she kept touching the space where a wedding ring would be—and that told her Ali might be in the market for her own second act.

Didi didn't know what had given Ali that wistful look in her eye when no one was watching. But Sea Turtle Resort had a way of fulfilling dreams even if you didn't know exactly what you were dreaming of.

Twenty

ALI

The morning after the Grand Finale, Ali decided to take Erica and Henry up on the offer of coffee at the Morning Bell. She woke up rested and with a plan: a walk and a coffee date with her two new friends. Hopefully, it would fortify her with the strength to push Didi. Ali's mission was to find facts, but she kept finding ways to relax a little longer before getting down to business.

This morning, though, the beach was the top priority.

She noticed, happily, that the fatigue that had been weighing her down for as long as she could remember was gone or displaced somehow. Ali had loose ends everywhere—her marriage, her career, and this place—but those ends were slightly less frazzled than if she'd been at home.

Was it the salt air doing its magic? She was beginning to see how people decided to chuck it all and open a seaside restaurant!

"When in Rome," Ali said to no one in particular. She found her leggings, her lightweight zip-up hoodie, and the University of Toledo ball cap she'd packed. It was time for a walk on the beach.

It was early, which suited her fine since she was an early bird. It seemed like she was always rushing in the morning: the kids' lunches, a meeting for Frogtown, a mammogram she needed to arrive at fifteen minutes before, or an errand to the store because they didn't have anything in the fridge for dinner. Always rushing.

This morning felt slower. The beach made it so. She locked the little Key Lime unit and palmed her key. And then she was off. No phone, though the view was something to capture. She always answered whenever her sisters or her kids called or texted her. Maybe it was time to try not being so tied to that phone.

Nothing was so urgent that it couldn't wait until after her walk on the beach. Who knew when she'd get this chance again? She had her Hokas on, the only shoes that really handled her intermittent plantar fasciitis, but then she thought better of it.

Get your toes in the sand, said a voice in her head.

Ali placed her shoes neatly by the front mat on the porch of the cottage. Each cottage had its own little front deck, all facing the ocean. They were in various stages of disrepair. Some needed a little sand and paint, others probably ought to be torn down, but this one, the Key Lime deck, was solid.

Ali stepped out on the path; all the cottages had an individual path that merged into a circle that led out to the beach.

Follow the yellow brick road...

Ali put her foot down on the sand and decided to hang a right for her walk. There were other walkers and runners dotted up and down the shoreline, but not many.

It was as if she had the place to herself. She supposed in another two months, it would be Grand Central Station, but right now, well, this was her private paradise to borrow.

Ali took a slow, deep breath. The sea salt air was divine. If she could bottle that up and take it home, she'd do it!

She decided to walk closer to the water's edge. For a while, she walked with her head down, eyes on the sand. The surf gently washed in and then out. She supposed there were days when it roared in and ripped out. She'd like to see that.

But today, it was a hypnotic and gentle motion as the water smoothed the sand over and over.

As she walked, scatterings of seashells caught her fancy. Most were broken or crushed.

But then a different sort of shell caught her eye: bigger, whiter, and more perfect than the rest she'd seen.

She picked up a conch shell that didn't have a single chip on it. She rinsed it in the seawater and decided to keep it. Maybe it would be her one souvenir from her strange solo trip to Haven Beach.

A few feet more and a white shell stood out from the rest. She decided that it would look lovely on her nightstand. It was practically begging her to collect it! After walking a little ways longer, Ali realized both her pockets were rather filled with her seashell finds.

Next time, she'd bring a bag. *Next time?*

A burst of cold shook her out of her improbable "next time" thought. The little foam of the waves had rushed over her feet. She skipped out of the reach of the waves and more toward the shore.

What's the fun in that, Ali Kelly?

Ali Kelly was not, in the parlance of self-help, connected to her inner child. She had too many outward children, from Jerry to her actual kids, to manage. But that inner child was activated by that sandy beach, and she shut off the impulse to stay dry and angled herself closer to the water.

Now, with each step, she was in the wet sand, her toes were covered, and then the next step, a whoosh of the water washed them clean.

She was playing like she was a kid. Or how she imagined it must be to play. Had she ever?

Her sisters would love this—*Ooh, and the kids*! She wondered if they were interested in coming down here sometime for spring break. Did soon-to-be divorced moms take their college-aged kids to spring break? What was the protocol for that?

Ali moved on in her mind. She didn't want to cloud this walk. Not when the new sun was soft butter yellow in the sky, and the sound of a seagull seemed unreal, foreign to her Midwest ears, but exactly what you'd expect on a beach.

She didn't know how long she walked or how far but thought it might be a good idea to turn around. The Key Lime Cottage and the Sea Turtle Resort was back the way she came, easy to find again.

Ali looked out at the water this time, on her stroll back, instead of down at the shells. She had no more places to put shells, so this was a better plan.

The water sparkled. She kept her eye out for dolphin fins, but none appeared. Instead, a metal gray pelican with a massive wingspan swooped back and forth. It dipped in front of her and flew behind her. She watched as it circled and then dove straight down into the water. Beak first.

"Breakfast, eh?" she said out loud to the pelican.

Who am I? Talking to pelicans!

Her foot didn't hurt. Apparently, a barefoot walk on the sand did wonders for plantar fasciitis.

Her feet led her right back to the Sea Turtle Resort.

The Key Lime waited, ready to welcome her back. Ali realized she was smiling. All by herself, no one was around, and she was smiling from ear to ear at the sight of the sweet little cottage and the resort property.

This place had something. She couldn't put her finger on it. Still, the entire time she'd worked at the Frogtown Convention Center, she worked hard to make it a community, a hub of people who enjoyed being together. She believed in an unseen "feeling" of a place that made it special.

That something special, that spark, was here. She felt it but couldn't define it. Maybe it was Didi and Jorge who cultivated the vibe here. Right now, though, it was just her and the cottage and the sand in her toes.

Vibe or not, it was time to get coffee, get information, and get some answers.

Ali placed her bare feet on the wooden steps of the little deck outside the Key Lime. The deck was warm, the planks grounding her, welcoming her back.

She did have a job to do, but before she did it, Ali carefully laid out her shell treasures, one next to another, on the rail of her tiny deck.

The act felt like meditation.

Twenty-One

ALI

The Morning Bell was only two blocks away from the Sea Turtle in the opposite direction from the Seashell Shack and across Gulf Boulevard.

It was easy to find.

A mango orange tin awning wrapped around the teal rectangle building. An unserious font on the purple bell-shaped sign that hung from the top of the building let you know this was the Morning Bell.

If the riot of color didn't make you happy, the smell of the coffee would.

Ali giggled and inhaled the aroma of roasting beans and cinnamon buns.

She stepped inside, and the eclectic array of colors and objects made it hard to decide where to look first!

The walls were decorated with old photos, some black and white, and some an orangey cast from the '70s. There were a few old maps framed as well. The walls themselves were '70s, a *Brady*

Bunch-style rec room paneling. And if it wasn't moving, it was painted mango.

The chairs and tables were orange, too, set in stainless silver metal frames.

If they weren't vintage, they were made to look so and quite successfully. Despite the vintage feel, the place was bright and clean, and nothing felt neglected about the way this place ran.

An intentional, relentless cheer was clearly the hallmark here.

A long high-display counter featured pastries of all kinds, several quiche options, and then, of course, a list of coffees to enjoy.

Erica emerged from the kitchen and clocked Ali immediately.

"Ali! Yes! So glad you made it. I sent Henry outside to the corner table I reserve for VIPs."

She was hardly a VIP, but it was sweet for Erica to say.

"What's your favorite coffee?"

"Oh, wow, I'm open to all kinds as long as it's not decaf."

"Right? Same. How about a flight?"

"A flight?"

"Yes, Morning Bell specialty. We have five little half cuppers and your favorite roast is the one you can order tomorrow."

"Lovely."

"Okay, which five?" Erica asked.

"Surprise me with the variety you like, I'm easy."

"I sensed that about you, hussy."

Ali laughed.

Something about Erica reminded Ali of her sisters. She had no artifice and no filter. Ali wanted to be more like that because it was a terrific recipe, in Ali's opinion. Erica also seemed so relaxed about her gig running a coffee shop. Though caffeine was her commodity, chilled out was her vibe.

Ali's smile continued as she located Henry at the corner table. They were outdoors under a canopy that protected customers from the heat of the sun but let them look out at the sidewalk, as walkers, bikers, and cars rolled by. It was the perfect place to people watch.

Henry stood up when Ali approached and gave her a cute little bow. Men never stood when a lady entered a room or joined a table! She'd seen it in old movies but couldn't remember experiencing that. It seemed like a thing of a bygone era, but it was delightful, Ali decided. Henry must have been more southern than she realized.

"Mornin'! I'm sorry I was on the phone and missed you coming in!"

"Hello. Don't worry, it gave me a chance to peek in there. Wow, how cute is it? Do you all just have cool vibes distributed to you when you open a business here or is it like an ordinance required for operating a business in Haven Beach? 'Must have cool vibes to open here'?"

"Ah, yes, we take a class at the Y, *Cool Vibes for Small Business Owners*. They also teach QuickBooks, so it's a twofer."

Ali giggled at his joke. "Brilliant." It was so lovely to meet people and gel with them.

But she did have an ulterior motive. And that was information gathering.

In short order, Erica appeared at the table with a tray in hand. She expertly weaved in and out of the increasingly busy outdoor eating space. She deposited the flight in front of Ali.

"Butter Blend, Oo La Leche, Uppers, ChocoLady, and Means Business. You'll like at least one of these because they run the table of flavors."

"Wow. Looks and smells wonderful!"

"And Henry, I've got your usual Boring Ass Coffee."

"She makes 'em all herself," Henry told Ali. "And yes, Boring Ass Coffee, that's the actual blend name. I'm afraid it fits me to a t." He paused, giving Ali the once over. "So, Ali Kelly, you look more relaxed than that first night at the restaurant. Our little patch of paradise agreeing with you?"

"Yes, of course, the beach naps I'm taking are sort of alarming. I never doze off like that at home!"

"You do that when you need it," Erica pointed out. "I remember when I first got here, I wanted to do yoga on the beach and kept falling asleep during Shavasana. The thing is, your body needs the sleep and then when it catches up, the naps are fewer."

"Yeah, same at The Shack. I thought I was going to be doing this gourmet seafood thing, and it was like the fish itself said, 'No, slow your roll, it's not that serious.' The beach told me, I didn't tell it." Henry took a sip of his Boring Ass Coffee.

Ali tried not to stare. *They sure did make them handsome in, where was it, South Carolina?*

"Remember you had that four-layer caviar dip on the menu?" Erica piped up. "I tried to tell you."

"I had to get over myself a bit."

"Our baseball star had Michelin stars in his eyes. It took him a while to understand we don't worry about that kind of thing here." Henry laughed at Erica's description of him.

"Michelin stars are a bit out of my wheelhouse, too," Ali said.

Ali's job at the convention center was adjacent to the hospitality industry. Toledo did not have a Michelin star; the closest place that did was Chicago, some four hours by highway.

"Yes, well," Henry conceded, "that was an aggressively career-oriented time of my life."

"How did you wind up here?"

Henry shifted in his seat and looked down for a beat. Ali felt instantly guilty that she'd stepped into something too personal. She'd felt at such ease with these two that she'd forgotten for a moment that she'd just met them.

"Ah, took it over from my brother."

"My ex."

Ali looked from Henry to Erica. They did seem almost like brother and sister from completely different parentage. Now she knew why.

"Yes, he opened the place here, and it was a bit of a mess. While I was chasing good reviews and fame and fortune, he was slinging daiquiris and uh—"

"Sleeping around?" Erica interrupted. "Yeah, not the greatest marriage. But I did get a bestie out of it!" Erica punched Henry on the shoulder.

"Hey, watch it. I don't want to spill a drop of the nectar of the gods."

"Anyway, when his brother, my ex, split during our contentious divorce, Henry came down to help clean up the mess."

"And I never left. Like you said, there's an ease here that lulled me from the get-go. I bought my brother out and retooled Seashell Shack."

"His purchase gave my ex enough to comply with the divorce settlement. And we all lived happily ever after!"

"Not the kind of bedtime story we were raised with, eh?" Ali said. "I can relate to relationship messes, I'll say that."

"When it rains, it pours." Erica put a hand out and patted Ali's.

It was like they had a bond. A cheating husband bond. Ali wouldn't wish it on anyone. Still, it was somehow comforting to know someone as vibrant and cool as Erica could also be not enough for some man who likely wasn't her equal by a mile.

Ali realized she was harboring a lot of doubt that what Ted had done was her fault. That she was the weak link, and he'd had no choice but to cheat.

But it wasn't her fault. Well, the marriage failing might have been a two-way street, but the cheating? That was at Ted's feet and his alone.

"So now you're here, and you own The Turtle!"

"Yeah, for a second anyway. If I can get Didi to give me the contact info of the management company, I can get appraisals going and, well, all the things needed to list it." She saw a look go from Erica to Henry.

"You're sure you're selling?" Henry asked.

"Yes, I'm not a resort manager or hotel baron. I'm a convention center assistant manager; actually, a former assistant manager. Between me and my two sisters, we can sell this for what, a couple of hundred thousand, and each one of us can get a little bump on our future retirement savings. That's the plan."

Henry and Erica were quiet for a second, upon hearing Ali's mission. She supposed it was natural. They'd just met her, and with Ali's plan, who knew what would happen to Jorge and Didi. It was hard not to love the old couple and here she was, about to sell the place out from under them.

Henry stepped in and filled the awkward silence. "Nothing wrong with that, very sensible. Though…it seems like event convention center manager is actually pretty close to what they need there at The Turtle."

"Yeah, it's a shame," Erica agreed. "Didi and Jorge are just not able to bring the magic like they used to."

"You mean because of his hip?" Ali asked.

"Yes, and she's older too now. It's a lot of work. But I'll tell you, that place is magic. I will never forget the nights I've spent on that beach with a glass of wine," said Erica.

"And those lights she put up for my fiftieth birthday? I mean, it was a *night*," Henry said. The two of them laughed, sharing some memory. Ali wished she'd been there and she'd just met them both.

"Well," Ali said, "I'm sure whoever buys it will fix it up, and you'll have those nights again. While I have the two of you, though, Didi has been a little hard to pin down. Do you happen to know the name of the management company they use? In case she's still unable to find her paperwork?"

"Honestly, I have no idea. I've never seen anyone but the two of them over there," Erica replied.

"Right. But, you know, I have a person you should talk to on the appraisal front. I think you'll find the numbers are a lot different than a couple hundred thousand," Henry said.

"Yeah, worse. You may be right. There are some major repairs needed. And there are only like two guests booked right now. Watch me owe on this thing."

The two old friends exchanged another look, and Erica piped up. "Ha, well, Henry will steer you right on a good agent. Patsy, right?" Erica looked at Henry, and he nodded. "You shouldn't decide anything until you know all the facts."

"Yes, like how in the world did we own this all this time and not know it? It's the craziest thing."

Her two new friends both muttered noncommittedly and buried their heads in their coffees.

Ali had the distinct impression they knew more than they were saying.

She may not have gone to the Y's *Cool Vibes for Small Business Owners* classes, but she did have the sense to let the topic trail off.

She was the outsider here, and she was about to upset their groovy vibe.

Twenty-Two

ALI

Ali had planned to get right to the point with Didi.

But Didi did not have the time to chat. There was excitement at the Sea Turtle. Ali found Didi in the laundry room in a cloud of fabric softener sheets and reciting to do lists to herself.

Ali grabbed the laundry basket, filled with hot towels, from the grateful Didi.

"We've got two families, one checking into the Mango Mansion, and I think I'll put the other in the Blueberry."

Ali's confusion was likely written clearly on her face.

"Mango's the one directly across from the Key Lime; its Mango color gives it away."

Ali thought about the cottage across from the Key Lime. It was not mango or even orange; it was weathered gray with pealing peach paint. And "mansion"? Well. Not so much. But the names of the cottages were part of the charm. She itched to get a scraper and a few gallons of mango-colored paint and do a once over before any guests arrived. The Blueberry was easy to figure, and its paint chips were less obvious. The darker blue was more forgiving. But the guests were coming today. There wasn't time for DIY upgrades.

Ali followed a busy Didi as she pulled heavy wet towels from one of the washers to transfer them to the now-empty dryer.

The wall of four washers and four dryers constituted a mini laundromat really. There were two more empty spaces, likely the ghosts of appliances past. If the resort was fully booked, there would be a need for all six. But as it stood now, with one family in the hotel and none in the cottages, four was three too many.

Didi was breathing heavily, Ali noticed. And it was no wonder. It was already warm by 10 a.m. The older woman was moving fast, trying to get the linen done—and who knows what else needed to be managed before the guests checked in.

"Here, let me help you. We can work and talk, if that's okay."

"You're the boss!"

Ali had a hard time accepting that fact. She still knew precious little about how that was possible. "Okay, yes. I guess I am. Give me that." Ali finished adding the towels to the dryer.

"The sheets for the bed are already in there. While these dry, I need to do a once over with the cleaning. Let me get the cleaning cart."

"I'll get it." Ali was done pretending she didn't own this place; she did, and she needed to take charge, at least until they sold it.

She knew she still needed to understand what she might owe Jorge and Didi. She needed to find out if there were any debts associated with the place. Was insurance up to date? Her brain, used to handling details, was kicking back in. She'd had enough strolls on the beach and naps. It was time to wake up and get it sorted.

Didi led the way, and Ali carried the gear. She used the old-fashioned key and opened up Mango Mansion. It did not smell great. Not bad, but also not fresh.

"It's been closed up for a bit."

Ali wondered when there had last been guests here. She

scanned the room. It was the mirror image of the Key Lime but slightly worse off. The draperies were stained, the furniture looked beat up, and the floor probably needed replacing. She noticed a few rag rugs on the floor and decided against moving them to see what was underneath. That was a reality check she didn't have the strength for at this point.

This cottage, like hers, was a one-bedroom, one-bath affair with a pull-out couch in the seating area and a queen bed in the bedroom.

"Oh," Didi said suddenly, "I don't know if you realized this or not, but we actually have an outdoor shower on this one and yours, kind of a fun thing. Maybe you should try it!"

Ali decided the bathroom was the first order of business, and told Didi so.

"Sure," Didi agreed. "I'm going to get these sheets changed, you work on the commode!"

"Sounds good."

Ali opened the bathroom door, and two little geckos skittered across the linoleum. She let out an involuntary squeal.

"You okay?" came the question from Didi.

"Yep, fine. Fine."

The geckos disappeared to a corner, and Ali wondered if she should hunt them down and relocate them or deal with the state of the bathroom.

Which...wasn't good.

The toilet seat was clean but old, and the sink was water-stained. Worse, it was unstable. It rocked like it might separate from the wall when she put a hand on it.

The medicine cabinet mirror was pitted, and when she opened it, the rusty hinges creaked.

None of these issues were present in the bathroom of the Key Lime. She started to wonder if the other four cottages were like the Key Lime or like the Mango.

Ali got out a bleach wipe and wiped every surface. There was a high little window. She used every muscle in her body to open it and get new air in the space.

After a few minutes she had wiped every hard surface in the room, but it didn't look any better.

The bathtub shower unit needed a new shower curtain, and a new towel rack, for that matter.

Is there time to make a run to Costco? What rate did Sea Turtle Resort charge for the Mango? What was the overhead for each unit's utilities?

Ali was doing calculations in her head and trying to estimate if she could get this place slightly better before the guests arrived as she went to find Didi in the bedroom.

"Didi, the bathroom isn't as clean as it should be. I—"

Ali stopped mid-sentence when she saw the normally constant motion Didi sitting on the bedside. She had her hands on her knees, and her head was down.

"Didi!" Ali rushed to her side and kneeled. She put a hand on Didi's.

"I'm sorry, just got a little overheated. I should have checked this room earlier. Jorge told me it was on his to-do list. And now the guests will be here in a little while."

Ali didn't like Didi's color. Her face was red, but her hand was cold.

"Didi, do we need to call 911?"

"No, no, just need a moment."

Ali walked into the kitchen and found a glass from the cabinet next to the sink. She ran the cold water, and a strange coughing sound spirited from the tap. *Ah, no, not great.*

"Didi, I'm walking you to the office. You're sitting there with a cold glass of water."

"The guests!"

"I'll handle that. And if your color doesn't improve, you'll have zero choice, I'm calling 911."

Didi didn't argue. Ali and Didi walked back toward the office.

Didi held Ali's elbow, and they took baby steps. Ali deposited Didi with Jorge, who took over.

"You did too much. Come on now, honey. Sit down and sip that water Ali got for you." His voice was tender, and the concern in his eyes for his wife at once broke Ali's heart and gave her hope.

She'd told Didi she'd handle things, so handle them, she would!

"If you need anything, just holler," Didi said, and Jorge nodded in agreement.

She waved them off. Ali usually hosted one hundred vendors descending on Frogtown with their displays, staff, products, and special requests. They all usually ignored sign-in times and showed up at the same time. Two small families would be no big deal.

A quick look around the office and Ali had her bearings. She found a list of what guest amenities the Sea Turtle offered. She made a quick decision. The Mango was in no way ready, and she couldn't get it ready. But there were six cottages. At least two had to be decent enough, and the best should be for the guests.

In less than twenty minutes, she'd moved herself out of the Key Lime and deposited her stuff in the office. She'd sort out her own living situation later. She only needed one more night anyway.

Ali knew the Key Lime was in much better condition than the Mango. Guests deserved the best Sea Turtle Resort had to offer. Even though what it had to offer wasn't at its best.

And she'd explain to the guests that repairs meant they couldn't stay in the Mango.

In Ali's run-through of options, the Blueberry had looked and smelled the best. If the décor was tired, well, that's just the way it was. Ali assumed that the families who rented here had to have some idea what they were getting. Plus, the Key Lime sat slightly in front of the Blueberry. Jorge told her it usually earned slightly less rent since it was a few more steps to the beach.

She checked on Jorge and Didi, who were both under an

umbrella by the green-looking swimming pool. Ali hoped that wasn't the big draw because it was clearly un-swimmable. She made a note to investigate who to call on that. Clearly, selling this place with a viable swimming pool would add value. For now, the priority was checking in the guests and making sure Jorge and Didi made it to retirement.

"Both of you, drink that water and stay out of the sun."

"You're going to have to give them keys. The phone number sheet, the schedule, and the maps are all in the cottages. And just tell them the pool is under construction," Jorge advised. He was calm. His trust in her was helpful. Didi, however, was agitated.

"What about the Grand Finale? I need to run to the store to get—"

"Didi, you need to not have heat stroke," Ali said. "I'll handle the Grand Finale. You handle yourself. Well, Jorge, handle your woman!" She winked at Jorge and they exchanged a look. He would handle his wife and be sure she was okay. She sensed he was grateful for her help. That made her happy and put her in a wonderful frame of mind for the guests' arrival.

It was five to four, showtime!

Twenty-Three

ALI

The Hafner family and the Noble family rolled into the parking lot at 4 pm sharp.

Two couples and a total of five kids piled out of two minivans that looked like they'd driven across the country.

Ali put her hostess face on. After years of hosting major conventions for the City of Toledo, she knew how to make people feel welcome, cared for, and special.

She poured that experience into greeting the Hafners and the Nobles.

"Welcome to Sea Turtle Resort!" She put on a smile, and it was only fake for half a second. Seeing the families warmed her heart.

The Hafners looked to be in their early thirties. The mother looked tired, but she was surprisingly pulled together having been in a family van for who knows how long. Her long wavy blonde hair and cute leggings had Ali feeling bad about the state she'd arrived here in. Mrs. Hafner was adorable. Two elementary school aged boys trailed behind her, also blonde, and there was a little brown-haired toddler girl on her hip.

Ali remembered those days, never a free hand.

The Nobles were also lugging two little ones, a boy and a girl, both in elementary school. Mrs. Noble and Mrs. Hafner looked like sisters. The kids all looked related, too.

"Let's get you checked in," Ali said brightly.

"I'll wait out here with the crew," said Mrs. Hafner. The other three adults followed Ali into the office.

"The office is also our laundry if you have any stuff to wash over the next few days," Ali said.

Ali registered the guests and explained they'd be in the Key Lime and the Blueberry.

"Unfortunately, the pool is out of order right now, but the beach is always in ship shape. As an apology for the inconvenience of the pool, I'll bring some breakfast tomorrow morning, if you're interested. The Morning Bell has the best donuts around."

They all seemed unfazed by the news about the pool. *Phew, good.*

While checking them all in, Ali learned Mrs. Noble and Mrs. Hafner were sisters.

"What a fun family vacation!" Ali said and was a bit wistful. She and her sisters should have done this when Faye's and her kids were little. They never had.

"While the laundry is open during business hours and if you have an emergency laundry need, just holler. I'm aware that with one, two, three, four, five," she playfully pointed to each kid, who giggled as she did it, "laundry emergencies happen."

The two moms looked relieved to hear it.

Ali had found a cart for luggage in the office and rolled it out after they finished checking in.

"I think we can get it all on here," she said.

"Are you kidding? We packed enough to move in," Dale Hafner said as he stacked his luggage on the cart. Brock Noble did the same. There was a little left in each van, but for the most part, the bulk of the luggage was loaded. Ali took a deep breath and started to pull the cart. It was a bumpy ride, but it was what these weary travelers deserved. This was their vacation.

"You're new here," Doreen Noble said as the families tumbled into the Blueberry and the Key Lime.

"Yes, just helping out a bit. You've been here before?"

"This is our third time. We come off-season, and honestly, with the prices, this is the only place we can swing with both families. Everywhere else are impersonal condos five flights up or at the resorts. Even with the meal plans, well, Dale's an electrician, I do nails, Brock is laid off, and Kerry is trying to work from home. We'd have to be millionaires to stay at those places."

Ali hadn't tried to book a family vacation in a while. She wondered if that was the case, that Sea Turtle Resort was unique?

It gave her a new perspective on the worn-down, out-of-date resort.

"I'm sorry we had to move you from the Mango. I know that's what you'd requested, but it is undergoing some maintenance."

"Oh, we're cool. The ocean is right there." Dale said, and he took in the scene.

"Grand Finale still same bat time, same bat station?" Brock asked.

"Sure is!" Ali answered confidently but realized she'd need to get moving on that immediately. The sunset was only two hours away.

"Ugh, did I forget sunscreen? How did I forget sunscreen?" Kerry said as she rifled through bags and her kids bounced around the Blueberry.

"I'll see you all at the Grand Finale."

Ali got out of the way and let the families start their vacations. She made a note to herself. She should stock the cottages with some amenities like sunscreen and shampoo. Maybe a few things that you couldn't fly with, too.

Ali shook her head; no, she shouldn't do anything. She was selling this place.

The two families she'd just met deserved to have a lovely vacation, though. They were working hard. She remembered the hectic days of having little ones, too, while working. They didn't need to know this might be the last hurrah for the Sea Turtle Resort.

Ali found Jorge and Didi sitting in the chairs by the fire pit. They looked a little better but also tired.

"Are the guests all set?"

"All set. Your instructions were perfect, and they're happily unpacking and looking for their sunscreen."

"Good," Didi said. "I'll get over to the market for the Grand Finale."

"You'll do no such thing, either of you." Ali had decided if she was in for a penny, she was in for a pound.

"The Grand Finale is a staple, part of the magic, we have to."

"I'm aware. I was enchanted with that bit of magic. But you're both tired. Let me, for one night, handle your Grand Finale duties."

"Jorge, this is too much to ask her. We need to get to the market and—"

"—You didn't ask," Ali interjected. "And I'm the owner, so technically, the boss. I need you two at top form when I head back to Ohio. While I'm here, you should recharge, at least for tonight."

"She's right," Jorge said to Didi. "Thank you, Ali. Didi tends to run herself ragged."

"But I love taking care of our guests."

"I know you do, I do, too, but we need to get you home. Start fresh tomorrow." Jorge looked at his wife with love and concern.

Ali nodded. He was speaking reason.

"I'm sure I can manage one night," she reassured them.

"Now, get going," Jorge told Ali. "Charcuteries don't make themselves!"

"Oh, for goodness' sake, it's a cheese board," Didi said, but while she protested, she allowed Jorge to take her hand and lead her toward the door.

"You've been doing my job and your job for too long. Let Ali do them for one night."

"But she's one person!"

"Yeah, and she's half our age, so the math works out."

Ali wasn't half their age, but those thirty years or so did make a difference. She felt invigorated and had a fire under her at the challenge.

With the guests checked in, she thought it best to focus on the Grand Finale. She had been to two. Both times, locals had showed up. Ali didn't want to disappoint Erica or Henry and also needed to be sure the families were enchanted! Theme parks might have fireworks, but they had the beach and the best sunset on Earth.

Ali didn't spend much time thinking about why she wanted to do this; she simply didn't have time for it. Her favorite moments at Frogtown Convention Center were when her vendors were happy, and event attendees had smiles on their faces. Touches like Ruby's Hot Dogs or video game stations for bored kids made her events shine.

She'd pour that into today. It was only one day, and she did own the place, after all. Why she owned it was still a mystery, but one she also didn't have the time for with the guests and the sun moving across the sky.

She needed to get several charcuterie boards prepared.

Didi had told her about the local produce and cheese market that she used so Ali could avoid Costco. Costco was great, but she wanted something unique and, more importantly, fast. A drive into Tampa or wherever was not going to be fast.

Moe's Market was two blocks away. She would like to walk, but she needed too many ingredients to carry back, so she got in the Jeep and popped over.

Moe's was a little ramshackle, if she was being honest. There were no t-shirts for sale or sunscreen, like the Publix down the road, where you could buy pretty much anything you'd need, from lunch meat to a wakeboard.

Moe's was all meat, produce, cheese, and wine, thank goodness.

Ali loaded a cart with what she'd seen on Didi's cheese board the night before. Then she searched for a few things the Hafner and Noble kids would like. Nothing fussy or pretentious but still special. They'd need cookies and grapes, and she thought crackers for the kids would be good.

"Can I help you find something in particular?" A man wearing a Moe's t-shirt, not very tall, but very muscular, she noticed, offered her a smile and his assistance.

"Oh, hello. Ah, actually, yes, crackers, some for grown-ups and some for little ones. The little ones need to be like Ritz but ritzier." She figured the kids would be happy with them.

"Aisle 6, let me show ya what we've got."

She followed and he listed a few options. "Here, these are like, elevated Ritz crackers. The kids will love them." He handed her a box, and she put it in the cart.

"Thank you." At this point, her cart looked full. The only thing she didn't have was a few cookies or sweet treats. She had fruit, but kids didn't always go for that.

Maybe I can hit Erica up for some sweets?

"Here, let's get you checked out. So, word travels fast. You're the new owner of the Sea Turtle."

"I am. Well, technically I've been the owner for a long time, but I only just found that I owned it. That's more accurate."

"Ah, that's quite a discovery! Well, rest assured the Riveras have done a lovely job in your stead. Even if you didn't know it was in your stead."

"Yes, they're wonderful. Just trying to lift the burden a little today for the Grand Finale."

"Ah, so you're going to need a few pastries. I'm going to call Erica and be sure she brings some along."

My thoughts exactly. "Oh, thank you, that's wonderful. So, how long have you been here at Moe's?"

"I'm Kent Churchill. Moe was my grandpa, so I've been helping out here for my entire life, with about a fifteen-year detour in Seattle."

"Do you know who owned the Sea Turtle before, say, the 1980s?"

"Can't say that I do, but don't Jorge and Didi?"

"Ah, they just work with a management company, which I also can't track down."

"Well, you can always go to the county. I happen to know that any property records, deed transfers, and what not are sketchy before 2006 around here. Trust me on that. Tried to add a loading dock back there. Confusion over who owned about twenty feet took me more time to sort than I care to admit."

"So, how did you sort it, if I may ask?"

Kent scanned her items and gently placed them on the short conveyor belt. "County records are at the admin building. It's on Palmetto Road. They should be able to look it up. Mine was on microfiche. But I did find them and prove that I did actually own my parking lot. Thank you, Grandpa Moe! He owned the next-door neighbor's parking lot, too. Which is in my back pocket for a drive-through window I'm working on." He put a finger to his temple and tapped it.

Ali laughed and said, "Thanks for the info, I appreciate it."

"Of course, the mom-and-pop owners around here have to stick together. Essential to survival with all the big condo Godzillas."

"Oh, I'm really here to just settle this up. I live in Toledo." Ali still didn't see herself as the owner.

"Ah, well, at least you're all set for the Grand Finale, and don't worry. I'll get Erica to rush some goodies over too. Don't want you left without sugar for the guests. It's their vacation!"

"Totally! Thank you again."

Ali made a mental note to pay a visit to the county offices and then hustled back to the Sea Turtle. She realized she didn't have a kitchenette anymore, thanks to giving up the Key Lime. She scanned the hooks on the wall behind the desk in the management office cottage.

Key Lime and Blueberry were taken, and Mango was a mess. That left the Lemon Love Shack, the Pink Lady, and the Strawberry something or other. From her earlier inspection, she knew the state of each of them. All the cottages had the same amenities, just some were in better shape than others. The Lemon Love Shack was the other cottage closest to the beach.

Well, let's give the Lemon Love Shack a whirl.

She loaded her grocery bags onto the luggage trolley, along with the trays she'd scrounged from the storeroom in the office and hoped for the best.

Ali opened the door of the Lemon Love Shack. The sun was golden now and it lit the place in a way the Instagram kids would envy.

"Wow, Golden Hour, I guess."

She didn't have much time. She surveyed the kitchenette and the table. She'd stocked everything she'd need to prepare the snacks. And before long, her charcuterie boards were looking respectable. A quick check in the cupboard revealed a nice big plastic bowl for the kids' crackers and snacks. She tested the little fridge, and while it seemed to be making a noise like it might give up at any moment, the interior was cold.

"Okay, hang in there a few more hours, please," she instructed the fridge.

She covered her snack boards with Saran Wrap and popped them in the fridge, doing a good once over to be sure there weren't any geckos also in residence. Satisfied that the Lemon Love Shack needed reno but not a demo, she stored her snack creations. Next she decided to look around the grounds for chairs and anything else the Grand Finale might need to make it special for the guests.

149

Ali walked into the courtyard of the Sea Turtle. Nothing to be done about the green pool, and the ocean horizon was the star anyway.

She roamed the little courtyard, picked up a few errant palm fronds, and realized the place also probably needed some major landscaping. Faye would go bananas if allowed to run amok in this little green jungle.

The fact was, Ali needed a real estate agent in here, soon. She needed an appraisal to decide how to proceed. Each broken-down piece of the place probably lowered its value. The more she looked, the more its disrepair revealed itself. Poor Jorge probably hated the idea that so much needed to be done. But it was a huge job for someone of his age. *Instead of feeling guilty that I'm going to sell*, Ali thought, *maybe I should consider that they'll be grateful. They're both past retirement age. Way past.*

Back in the office, Ali explored a big storeroom area. There were labeled bins and remnants of perfectly organized shelving and storage. But there was also a fair amount of chaos.

At every turn at the Sea Turtle, she could see how Jorge and Didi used to do things versus how they now seemed to be barely scraping by.

She could spend all day in the storeroom, organizing and sorting. But there was no time. The guests were here, and that had to be the focus.

Ali moved things around a bit and discovered just what she had in mind.

Lights!

Ali looked at her phone. There was enough time, she hoped, to do this little bit extra for the guests' first night. In short order, she sat on the ground in the courtyard with several tangled strings of white Christmas lights.

"Oh, how, ugh. Where's the end?" she grumbled to herself, or so she thought.

"Come again?"

Ali jumped a bit in her spot.

But it was only Henry, with several bottles of wine. "I brought the fun, see? No worries about having enough wine. I hear you're pinch-hitting on the Grand Finale."

"News travels fast. How'd you hear?"

"Moe told Erica, and she called me. You probably have it under control, but you know, a bottle of wine never hurts. And a co-pilot on your first Grand Finale, well, if you need one. I humbly offer my services."

He did a courtly bow, and Ali's frustration with untangling the Christmas lights turned to gratitude.

"I gratefully accept," she said and returned his bow with a regal nod and hand gesture.

"Okay, so you also need my expertise in the light department. That's painfully clear."

"Expertise?"

"I can reach the high branches."

"Ah, yes, that would be good since I have no clue where Jorge keeps the ladder."

Henry offered her a hand to help her up. She put her hand in his. And a frisson of attraction zipped through her like a shot of espresso. *Wow.* But Ali quickly shuddered that little distraction away. Number one, she had a husband—well, barely, but still, vows were vows, to her at least—and two, Henry wasn't hitting on her. He was being a good neighbor! She focused on the task at hand, the stupid tangled lights.

"Are you sure? It's maddening." She lifted the wad of bulbs toward her knight in sandy flip-flops.

"I can take it."

She gave him a wadded-up string, and he got to work. He had significantly more success with his strand than she did with hers.

"See, I've got skills."

"I got that one started for you," Ali replied.

The two had fun untangling the lights and stringing them

about the base of the palms in the courtyard. The irritation she'd felt at the start of her little light project evaporated into something like giddy fun. This was fun. This was the same fun as decking the halls for Christmas or creating a cool display in the convention center. She liked creating experiences, and it appeared Henry did too!

"I have to say, not something I thought I'd be doing on my fact-finding trip. But it looks incredible!"

The already charming common area of the Sea Turtle Inn was now twinkling in the late afternoon sun. *This is so cute!* It was no kingdom of magic one could experience in Orlando, but it was a little nook of magic, and she'd made it so.

"You have a good eye for creating beautiful things, just like Didi."

"That's a high compliment," Ali said, and she meant it. Didi, in short order, had made Ali feel like part of the Sea Turtle family. Even if the older woman wasn't up to the physical tasks that the place required, she'd welcomed Ali with open arms. The thought filled her with a spike of guilt. She was about to pull the rug out from under this little magic carpet ride.

Henry helped her get the food and chairs sorted and soon, Erica arrived with all manner of cookies for the kiddos.

"This is so helpful. What do I owe you both, truly? I appreciate this so much, and so will the guests."

"Girl, these are my extras," Erica said as Henry poured her a glass of white. "I let the staff take home a half dozen of whatever we don't sell so our cookies are always fresh. You're not paying for what I already give away."

"I will ask for payment on the wine," Henry added, "which includes me using the washer and dryer next week. Mine is on the fritz. I'm on my last three pairs of antique jeans."

Ali nodded. "Deal."

She looked toward the beach and then back to the little alcove of chairs and food and good people. For a brief moment, Ali allowed herself to imagine what a lovely life it would be, sitting here every night.

"Can we go in? Can we go in?"

Ali's imagination was interrupted by the laughter and pleas of the Hafner and Noble children hopping toward the water.

"You're kidding? You were in all day!" Doreen Noble shook her head, but Brock Noble stepped up. "I'll keep an eye. Let's go!"

The five cousins ran toward the water. Doreen, along with her sister Kerry and Kerry's husband Dale, approached the little spread of food and drink.

"Welcome to the Grand Finale," Ali announced. "White?"

Both moms nodded, and Dale decided on a beer, which Ali had set in a cooler. She was mindful of the fact that not everyone was a wine drinker. Her dad never let anything but Bud Light lubricate his downtime.

"Take a load off, ladies," Ali said, and the moms gratefully sat in the beach chairs. More beachgoers trickled toward them, and so did a few more local business owners.

Erica introduced her to a man who rented beach equipment, a woman who owned a hair salon a few blocks over, and then Kent Churchill from Moe's arrived.

They all greeted each other warmly and exchanged highlights of their day.

It was an informal business owner of Haven Beach get-together, and Ali got to be a fly on the wall. They talked about everything from a repaving of a nearby street to a new condo proposal for a vacant lot around the block.

"Oh, did you hear that Ford Taylor's house is set to be done this month?"

That caught her ear.

"Is that the Ford Taylor I think it is?"

"If you think it's the one who has a billion-dollar fashion and home décor line, then yes," Erica said.

"Wow." Ali was impressed. She'd met all these amazing business owners but none of them seemed like they were used to having billionaires in their midst.

"He bought two older beach cottages, side by side, tore them down—what, four years ago—and has been constructing a behemoth mansion. It's about a quarter mile that way," Kent explained.

"Yeah, I heard he may be living in it full time. A nasty divorce, his ex is getting—what did the tabloid say—oh yeah, their Manhattan apartment and some house in the Hamptons. So, he'll be homeless if he doesn't get the beach house done," Erica informed them.

"Well, I hope he likes crab cakes," Henry said. "I think my waitresses would appreciate tips from a billionaire."

The conversation moved on to other topics and goings on in Haven Beach. Ali made a mental note to look for the fancy house on her next beach walk.

And slowly, the idea of getting out of here tomorrow or the next day, morphed into maybe she'd need an extra week.

"Whoo hoo! Look, look!" One of the Hafner kids was pointing to the stunning horizon. A dolphin, as if on cue, breached out of the water and playfully splashed back down.

"Cheers to you." Henry clinked his wine glass in Ali's direction.

"What?"

"That dolphin was a pretty darn good finishing touch for your first Grand Finale."

"Oh, well, you know, I just let him know we wanted it perfect for our Sea Turtle guests," Ali joked.

The sunset and the assembled group of vacationers and locals clapped and cheered. The sunset did not disappoint, and Ali felt good that neither had the Sea Turtle, thanks to her work and a little help from her new friends.

Twenty-Four

TOLEDO 1982
Belinda

It broke Belinda's heart that Joetta was so far away. And that their parents didn't seem to care. Worse. They'd cut Joetta's existence out of their lives, their family, the minute she'd run.

It was so easy to eliminate her entire life from their home, the club, the stories they told.

Belinda knew people gossiped; they always did. Around the punch bowl, around the card tables placed far from their mother's, people whispered about Joetta's disappearance. Mommy said she was "abroad." And that was it.

As the years passed, the whispering about Joetta stopped. It was replaced by someone else's gossip.

Especially since there was no new fodder about where she was and what she was doing. No new grist for the mill. Fresh scandals were so much more fun than old rumors. Their parents were disciplined and stark. They had shut the door to Joetta.

That starkness was the threat that kept Belinda in line. She, too, could be cut from the picture just as easily.

Belinda did exactly as her parents expected. She lived up to their ideas of how a young lady should act, date, be, and talk. It was easy not to rebel or even have fun with the heavy heart that now sat in her chest. The Gulfside Girls were no longer, just a dull day-to-day life. Joetta was her joy, and it was painful to see that wasn't true for their parents.

Belinda finished high school, and she went to college, though she didn't really have a passion for any career or job. Her mission, expressed by Mommy, was to find a husband.

But just like not really caring what her job might be, she also didn't have any passion for any particular future husband. She went on dates, but Joetta had literally given up everything for a man. Belinda wasn't planning to do the same.

This was the source of the quarrel now between Belinda and her parents. They wanted her "married off" to someone they approved. Belinda avoided the questions even if she couldn't avoid the pressure her parents put on her.

Though, she had to put the brakes on, when her mother floated Banks Armstrong as a good match. Banks seemed to be the only one who remembered that Joetta existed.

"I know you're not supposed to talk about her," he said one day, "but can I ask you if she's okay? I think about that a lot. She is so trusting and open, and that can be dangerous."

She reassured Banksy. She stuck to the party line that she was traveling "abroad." Banks was a good guy. A good friend to Belinda. She hated lying to him, but he was the only one asking these days.

"She's happy, just done with us here in Florida. Don't worry."

But Belinda was not about to match up with Banksy, knowing that in his heart, he'd always love Joetta the most. Banks was now the second in charge at his family country club, and though she wouldn't "match" with Banks, Belinda was happy to work for him. She took her useless college degree and applied it to the country club. She was the social director. It was a career her parents approved of; she liked it, and Banks said she was good at it. She had no husband yet, but at least she'd be able to meet the "right kind of men," and so her parents approved her career path until she settled down.

In 1982, Belinda decided to take a big risk. Her parents were going on holiday in Europe for over a month. They'd be an ocean away. This was her chance to check up on her baby sister without getting permission or getting into a battle.

Belinda took the money she'd squirreled away from working as the social director of Armstrong Hills Country Club and flew to Ohio.

They'd talked only a dozen or so times on the phone. But they wrote to one another at least once a week. The letters were way easier. She had a post office box her parents didn't know about, and the sisters' letters came back and forth with regularity.

Belinda had learned all about the house in Toledo, her two nieces, and even had a few pretty pictures of the girls. In turn, Belinda sent money, clothes, and letters to keep their connection strong, despite what their parents intended.

When the opportunity of a month of unscrutinized time presented itself, Belinda took advantage of it.

It was a quick flight from Tampa to Toledo Express Airport on Air Florida. When she exited the small airport, her sister was there!

"Joetta!"

The two ran to each other. Two little girls trailed Joetta.

"Oh! Ali looks just like you! Hello, Ali! I'm your aunt!!"

"Hello."

Ali looked Belinda in the eye and nodded. She was so polite, it was hard to imagine the child was only eight. She was little but seemed to regard Belinda with a bit of skepticism. Smart, seeing as she was technically a stranger. Ali was the big sister; she was used to protecting her little sister. *This one is my kindred spirit*, Belinda thought.

"And you must be Faye."

Faye pushed her arm straight out to Belinda. In her little fingers were a cluster of yellow flowers. A moist paper towel was wrapped around the stems. "Here, I grew these all by myself. Black-Eyed Susans."

"I love these, Faye! You have a green thumb!"

"Come on, Mommy," Ali piped up. "The sign said ten-minute loading and unloading."

"Ali keeps us on track, all of us."

The comment worried Belinda. *Why would a child have to keep the mom on track?* It was a window into the life that Joetta was living.

Joetta's husband, Bruce Kelly, was the same stoic figure Belinda remembered. They greeted one another politely enough, though Belinda still didn't see the appeal. He was still every inch muscle and aloof detachment but now, he also had a few wrinkles around the eyes. There was a look of skepticism toward her that Ali had mimicked, clearly.

"Don't forget Wednesday is garbage day, and the cans have to be out before 7 am. That means the night before if you're unable to get up," Bruce instructed his wife.

Unable to get up? Belinda looked at Joetta.

"I get migraines," Joetta offered by way of explanation.

Ali stepped in and addressed her father. "Don't worry, Daddy. I'll be sure the cans get brung out."

"Brought out," he corrected her.

And Belinda thought again that her little niece was taking a role too old for her years. Taking the garbage out because Joetta might not be able to? That was just odd.

"She is everyone's helper," Joetta said and ran her hand over Ali's shiny spun gold hair.

"Auntie, come see my garden!" Faye grabbed her hand, and Belinda was led from the kitchen of the bungalow to the backyard. This was a relief; there was tension between her sister and her brother-in-law, and Belinda didn't want to be in the middle of it. All this time, Belinda had consoled herself that though she'd lost Joetta in their family, her sister was in a loving marriage and had created a happily ever after. But this didn't feel like a happily ever after.

She was grateful this visit coordinated with Bruce's yearly fishing trip with "the boys."

Belinda didn't know who "the boys" were and didn't care. What she cared about was time with Joetta and her babies. The tension she'd sensed would be gone as soon as he was.

And sure enough, as soon as Bruce left, the mood was better. Joetta was lighter, too. They had four whole days to just be together! They were going to shop and go to the pool and maybe see *The Secret of NIMH* at the movie theater.

One day, as the sisters "garage saled" in Joetta's neighborhood, several neighbors commented on how Joetta had a "good eye." Belinda was proud of her. Of course she had style! Even on Bruce's tight leash, Joetta had cute clothes and had decorated their little home with charming touches.

Yet Belinda observed that the formerly bold Joetta demurred at the compliments and deflected them.

"I just know how to sift through the junk," Joetta explained as the sisters walked arm in arm along Cheltenham, a street a few blocks from where Joetta lived. The neighborhood was called Old Orchard. The trees were tall and leafy green, so different than their Florida home.

Joetta described the lay of the land.

"This is the fancy part of the neighborhood we're in now, not as fancy as Ottawa Hills, but they do estate sales, not garage sales, so it's harder to get the good stuff there."

Ali and Faye rode ahead of them on a tricycle and a bike with training wheels. Belinda noticed that the girls looked like miniatures of Joetta and Belinda. Ali, a replica of Joetta, and Faye, with her wavy brown hair, a mini of herself.

"Remember riding bikes on Gulf before it got so busy?"

"I do, I miss that."

The visit was lovely, for the most part. And Belinda would have had nothing but fond memories to take back to Florida, except the last night spoiled the happily ever after idea, completely.

They'd baked cookies with the girls, stayed in, and just enjoyed each other's company. And, of course, had a few glasses of wine. Joetta poured too much, in Belinda's opinion. Her sister was tiny and seemed not to know how much was too much. Belinda remembered how poorly Joetta had handled beer all those years ago. But now it was wine, and it made her sister weepy.

"I just feel useless most of the time, you know. We never have enough money, and I'm always begging for pennies, but Bruce doesn't want me to work. Ha, though, what would I do for a job? I have zero skills, right? Getting a tan? That's not a hot commodity on the job market."

"Do you want to get a divorce? I can get a lawyer to you or—"

"No, no, I love Bruce. He loves me. I'm just feeling nostalgia, I guess. When getting a tan was our only job. I am so sick of housework, you know? Or no, you don't. Mommy and Daddy still have Erline and Barker, right? You don't have to clean a thing."

"Well, I've moved to the guest house, trial run for my own place, so I do clean that."

"Ha, the horror."

The edge on her sister was unmistakable. But it faded quickly as she started talking about the girls.

"Ali is so smart. Do you know she was reading these *Golden Books* before kindergarten? Bruce thought she was just memorizing what I'd read to her, but nope, he tested her. She was really reading before she ever stepped into Old Orchard Elementary School."

"She seems older than her years."

"Oh, she is, she's the little boss, no doubt." There was no edge on that, only pure love for her precocious daughter.

"And Faye and those flowers!" Joetta added. It seemed everywhere they went, Faye was either picking flowers or planting them. She loved being outdoors and collecting things from gardens and yards along the way.

"She's my tomboy, always with a scrape on the knee and dirt under her fingernails. I love that, though. Mommy would have a fit, you remember, if we had the slightest bit of mud on our jumpers?"

"I do remember."

The night finished with the wine, and Belinda was tired. She had a busy travel day ahead and was ready to turn in. Belinda had been sleeping on a pull-out couch on the porch, and after her three glasses of wine, she fell asleep hard.

She was grateful her flight wasn't until afternoon; her head was going to hurt!

But it was worth it to spend time with her sister.

In the middle of the night, in the depth of sleep, a thud and then the sound of glass breaking woke her up.

She oriented herself and stood up, quickly moving like a rocket toward the sound. *Is there a prowler? What if they're upstairs with the girls!* Belinda didn't think about her own safety, just her sweet little nieces. She ran toward the sound. Belinda wound up in the hall, outside Joetta's room.

There was no prowler. Belinda tried to process what she was seeing.

Joetta was on the floor of her bedroom. Blood was oozing out of her foot. A broken wine glass had shattered all over the wood floor of the bedroom.

"Be careful, Auntie, you don't have shoes on."

Belinda whipped around to see Ali, tennis shoes on, with a broom that had a dustpan on the handle in one hand and paper towels in the other. She walked around Belinda to Joetta.

"Mama, you need to be still. Here." The little girl set the broom against the bed. Carefully, she folded a sheet from the paper towel roll and put it on Joetta's cut foot. Joetta winced. "Mama sometimes has accidents when she has her headaches," Ali informed Belinda.

"Sure, how about I help her, and you go back to bed. It's so late." Belinda's heart was breaking for Joetta and even more for little Ali.

"I have to clean this up. She'll forget, and it's dangerous." Ali tilted her head to her mother.

"Okay, well, how about I hold the dustpan for you?"

"That would be nice. Thank you, Auntie."

The two helped Joetta back into the bed. The cut was small, thankfully, and the paper towel seemed to staunch the blood quickly. Joetta closed her eyes, seemingly unaware of the mess and that her daughter was managing it.

Belinda watched the beautiful, sweet girl efficiently wield the broom. Belinda dutifully assisted with each sweep of the broken glass.

"There, I think that's it," Belinda said. "You did a great job."

"Stand back, one more check."

Belinda stepped back as her little niece asked. She watched as Ali took her hand and gently glided it across the planks of the floor in light sweeping motions. With a quick intake of air, Ali looked at her hand. There was a tiny spec of blood in her index finger.

"See, missed a piece, they're hard to see. But they could cut Mama's feet."

Belinda nodded, acknowledging the pretty little girl's attention to detail.

Ali did another pass over the floor with the broom that was

taller than her. Her face was serious, her eyes focused on every inch of the floor.

Belinda tried not to cry.

She had to be at least as tough as her nieces.

Twenty-Five

ALI

Ali's management of the Grand Finale was still in her mind when she woke up. The smile on the little ones' faces as they ran up and down the beach was contagious. She'd caught a hit of their joy, and it woke her up this morning. Not a bad way to wake up!

Even more than the kids, she had given the parents, the families, a memory. Well, the gorgeous sunset had done that, but she'd gilded the lily, as they say.

Thanks to the location, a little snack, and good company, the sunset spectacular was its own fireworks at the park event. And there were no lines to get in or overpriced souvenirs to contend with.

Erica and Henry had showed up to lend their easy vibes and veterans' perspectives, and in the end, Ali was also glad to have given Jorge and Didi a night off. *Did they have an official backup? What would have happened if I wasn't here?* The questions added to the many that Didi needed to answer.

As wonderful as it all was, Ali realized she had a job to do for her own family now. It was time to see the books, time to get the real estate agents involved.

Didi had done that, at least. Put the books out on the desk for her to see.

Ali was used to budgets and schedules. This would be easily surveyed compared to all she had to manage for Frogtown, from payroll to building regs.

She opened the current year...and the imbalance was terrifying.

The bookings were down to a trickle.

She looked at the expenses of the operation.

Utilities, maintenance, taxes, and salaries for Jorge and Didi were listed. Their salaries were minuscule. *How in the world do they manage?*

Well, she did remember both were retired from other careers, so this was their "extra," maybe? But they were working full-time for a decidedly part-time income.

It was all managed from a central checking account.

They weren't in the red. They were even. She went back through a few years and did see that the rentals brought in so much more, even three or four years ago, but certainly, since the pandemic onward, things had gone downhill here.

She made a few notes.

To make Sea Turtle profitable would take so much work. Work that Jorge and Didi maybe just couldn't do anymore. She remembered the phone bill, unpaid, the calls unanswered. There was no website either, so no wonder no one was staying here. They couldn't, unless they had a reservation from a year ago or they walked up and tapped Didi on the shoulder for a rental.

Ali closed the ledgers. The math was easy here, and the job was hard.

Ali looked at her phone. It was just about time for her appointment with Patsy Gleaner, the Gulf Coast's Premiere Elite Commercial Real Estate Agent. Or so it said on her website, Gulf Coast Elite.

At 11 a.m. on the dot, a tiny woman knocked on the screen door of the office.

"Hello!"

Ali swung open the screen and let Patsy inside, though letting really wasn't what you did with this woman. You made way for her!

Ali was not tall, at 5'4", but she was long-limbed. Most people thought she was tall until they stood next to her. Patsy was maybe five feet? She was built like a gymnast and had the same flip-flopping energy. Her hair was a literal bouffant, though she didn't look much older than Ali. She wore white capri pants, high-heeled white pumps, and a leopard print blouse tied at the neck with a big bow. Her pink lipstick and nails matched perfectly, and she smelled like Elizabeth Taylor's Passion Perfume.

This little dynamo grabbed Ali's hand with both hers and shook hard.

"I'm so excited you called me! We've all had our eyes on this place for just ever. Ever!"

"You have?"

"Are you kidding? It's prime beachfront and no one had been able to touch it since God knows when. I've called the management company personally a dozen times over the year, but not even so much as a return call. And now there's not even a number."

Ali had found the same problem, and unfortunately, Didi and Jorge were no help either. They said it was all "on the internet."

"Well, be that as it may, I own it, it turns out, and I need to get a better picture of what it's worth."

"You own it? How amazing! Did you buy it? I didn't see a real estate transfer notice in the records? All under my nose! That's quite a feat."

Ali didn't feel like she owed Patsy her life story. As likable as the little dynamo was, they had just met. And Ali didn't really know the story herself. She decided to keep things vague.

"My father passed away recently; we discovered it while we settled all of his affairs."

"My condolences. Okay then, let's take a walk, shall we?"

"After you."

Ali gave Patsy a similar tour to the one Didi had given her just a few days ago.

"Oh gosh, this hotel, I mean, this was *the* place to stay back when I was a kid, in high school."

"Really?"

"Yes, before all the condos, we'd come for spring break when the *MTV Spring Breakers* came to Daytona. We had a much more chill vibe, but still, all the cute boys!"

Ali laughed; she liked Patsy.

"But, yikes, these rooms, ah, ew."

Ali had an urge to stick up for the little hotel. "They're okay, cleanish."

"Aha, but that doesn't cut it if you're going to get top dollar."

They walked through the little inn and then out to the pool.

"Whoa, what in the Sea Turd is this pea soup?"

"Sea Turd?"

"Yeah, sorry, love, just being honest. That's the nickname this place has, thanks to, uh, stuff like this."

Ali felt the instant urge to defend Didi and Jorge. "The managers have had to let a few things slide, health issues."

"I'd say this is supposed to be aquamarine, not gangrene."

"No, I mean *they* have health issues. I'm told it's a chemical issue with the pool, though, not structural." Ali said this and really didn't know if she was lying or not. She also really didn't know why she was taking this all so personally. She wanted an honest assessment of the value of the place. That was the job she was here to do.

They moved on to the cottages. The Hafners and the Nobles were heading out to the beach with various toys, blankets, and umbrellas.

"Wait, I didn't get your neck!" Kerry Hafner called after the youngest as he sprinted toward the surf.

Ali smiled. She remembered that same battle to baste her little ones in sunscreen when all they wanted to do was jump in the water.

"You saw the Inn had six units, and there is also a penthouse, but that's, uh, under construction." She lied; it was boarded up. She hadn't even been inside, but it did sound good, a penthouse.

Patsy had her iPhone out. She was making voice notes as they walked away from the pool to the beach cottages.

"Approximately two acres of frontage with one acre deep."

"I really love the cottages; I had the pleasure of staying in the Key Lime. It's really a Zen experience, you know?" Ali had grabbed the keys of all the vacant cottages so Patsy could see each of them. They all had a slightly different vibe, though the same amenities.

"Zen? No. No time for yoga in this market!"

As Patsy investigated the Mango, she pinched the fabric of her leopard print blouse and separated it a few times from her chest in an effort to fan herself. "Menopause is a real treat, and in Florida, my hot flashes are like someone left the sliding door open to hell itself, phew."

"Sorry, they have wall units, but we didn't think you'd need them on for this tour."

"I don't."

Patsy barely looked at the cottages.

They walked past the fire pit and out to the beach.

"This is the only thing that really matters."

"What?"

Patsy made another audio note on her phone. "Possibly fifty units, either rental or highest ticket. Check zoning."

"Fifty? No, it's six and then six over there."

"No, sorry, I forget my thoughts if I don't put them right into the notes app. Do you have the Notes app? It's a lifesaver. Another fun fact, my memory is doodoo these days. I just went on Estra-diol, though, so my doctor says it should start getting better. Here's my advice: get a woman OB/GYN. They know, you know?"

Ali nodded. *What the heck are we even talking about?*

"I know," Patsy said, "you're standing there thinking I'm two nuggets short of a six-pack, right?"

Ali laughed. "No, you're a lot, though."

"I get that. I am all me, all the time. No other way to be."

"I admire that, I'm working on it."

"You're what? Late forties? Your life is just getting interesting."

"That much is true. The last few weeks have been a whirlwind."

"I can see that. So, let's get down to brass tacks."

"Okay."

"This hotel and these cottages are tired, out of style, and a financial drain. Whoever owned this place held out so long that the market has moved on."

"I think they're so cute."

"Yeah, but you could be charging triple for a condo facility. If you're looking to do that. But that's also work work work, plus with the new building regs, it's not cheap."

"Nothing is down here, I noticed."

"Here's what I recommend. You give me this listing. The entire property. And we sell it for you. Likely, the developers will be able to tear it down, and do this right to maximize the rental income from vacationers. It's impossible to do that with this setup."

Ali felt defensive again. This place didn't need to be torn down. It just needed new energy.

"Condos on this stretch could go for millions per condo for the owners and thousands of dollars a week to them for vaca-tioners."

"Millions? Like two million?"

Patsy peered over her chunky animal print progressive glasses and leveled her most serious face at Ali. "I'd tell you to sit down, but we're on the beach, and I don't have my bathing suit. So, here's my no B.S. number. This land alone, the acreage? This can easily list for fifteen and sell for ten."

"Ten what?" Ali was starting to feel faint. *Are hot flashes contagious?*

"Ten million dollars in your pocket. You know, provided you own this free and clear."

Ali did want to sit down; her breath had got shallow. The conversation felt unreal. What did the kids say? She needed to touch the grass.

"You've got prime beach property, just not prime beach rental. Let me take this off your hands, and your next chapter will be as a millionaire. Well, a multi-millionaire."

Patsy Gleaner was a dynamo, and she had, with that information, given Ali a whole new picture of her future.

Twenty-Six

ALI

Ali tried to process the sheer magnitude of the numbers Patsy had quoted. The real estate agent had left her card and a palpable craving for the listing as she drove away.

Ali needed to talk to Faye and Blair. She needed her sisters' thoughts and support.

She'd sent them several videos and pictures of the hotel and the cottages. She also sent a photo of the bog-like swimming pool so they had the most realistic idea possible.

After a few texts, all three sisters got on Facetime together.

Ali had set up a foldable lounge chair under the largest palm at the side of the beach and popped in her earbuds. She still felt like all this was some sort of out-of-body experience.

Seeing her two sisters in the little boxes warmed her from the inside out. She had only been gone a week, but the last few months had been a blur from the trauma of losing their dad to her husband to all the upheaval of what they'd learned since.

It was so much; maybe too much. It all sat on Ali's chest right now and she had a hard time taking a deep breath. Seeing her sisters though, that was bringing her back to herself. They needed her. She needed them.

They'd sort this out, whatever this was.

"Well, how are things?"

"Cold and gray, the usual," Faye said. Ali could see her sister's kitchen in the background, with dozens of plants on every available surface. Her weapon against seasonal affective disorder was as many green things as she could find.

"Yeah, here too," Blair said. She was in a coffee shop in Cinci.

"Yeah, quite cold and icy here too," Ali joked as she pointed the camera to the beach and then back toward the little cottages.

"That's it. I'm officially jealous," Faye said.

"I can't believe Dad never told us this, never let us go there on Spring Break. That's so frustrating," Blair said.

But of the three of them, Blair had enjoyed the most stuff. Their father had indulged her, and they had too. Blair was their baby doll.

"Well, here's the bad news. The pool is in disrepair, the hotel needs an inspection and makeover, and the six cottages are all in some state of musty."

"But the beach!" Faye exclaimed, and she was right.

No matter how Ali tried to be practical, the spectacular here drowned out any talk of disrepair.

"It's calming and invigorating at the same time. I'm not going to lie."

"Any progress on how we came to be the owners?"

"Unfortunately, no. But the caretakers are adorable. I can't put my finger on why I connect so well with Didi, but I love her. Anyway, they're a little addled; this job is too much for them these days. That's clear. And they have never actually met anyone at the management company. So, I don't know who owned it before us or who even put the management company in place. Because ostensibly, they've been managing it FOR us for decades. They have an account they work from for expenses, their salaries, and taxes, and the surplus stays in the account."

"What the heck? Was Dad holding out on us? Does he have cash somewhere?" Blair asked.

"Not that I can see. No one has ever withdrawn from it, other than the caretakers for legit expenses that have gone right back to this business. There was a surplus, but the decline of this place has drained it."

"So there was money, once, and it's gone. Just our luck," Faye sighed.

"And it's operating on fumes right now," Ali continued. "The place isn't exactly teeming with people. Honestly, that's really only because it's so hidden. I did a little research. It's one of the last affordable ways for a family to stay on the beach around here, so it really could be fully booked if it was fixed up. Or if we got new management in here."

"What are you saying? Are you going into hotel management now?" Faye asked, her eyes wide.

"No, no, just what I found out doing the research. Though I will be sad to leave. It turns out I think I love it here." But she didn't think, she *knew*.

Ali had started to fantasize about coffee with her new friends in the morning and Grand Finales every night. She could envision how she'd decorate the cottages and entertain a wedding party. But it was a pipe dream. It really was a fantasy. She had a million loose ends in Toledo, and didn't everyone in the north fantasize about chucking it all to live on a beach? It was childish and impractical.

Still, Erica and Henry were doing just that. And Patsy's information had changed the equation entirely.

"Earth to Ali, hello?" Blair said.

"Sorry, sorry. So here's the reason we can't keep it. If we sell it, we're talking upwards of ten million dollars."

"Wait, my connection glitched. You did not just say what I think you said," Faye gasped.

"Holy Toledo!" Blair chimed in.

"Yeah, they'll tear it down, sell it to a condo company, and make three times that on condo sales and then rentals. Or a celebrity buys it, tears it down, and builds a mansion on the beach. Either way, it's life-changing money for us. Split in three, well, that's three million each, before taxes."

"Oh my gosh, oh my gosh!" Blair was waving her hands in the air like she was drying nail polish.

Faye appeared to have grabbed a pen and paper and was doing some sort of math.

"Look," Ali went on. "That's just an estimate from the real estate lady. So, yeah, do not pass go, do not collect two hundred dollars, go directly to the market."

"How fast would we get the money?"

"I don't have an answer for that, Blair, I've never sold a multi-million-dollar property."

"This is almost too much to process," Faye said.

"That's the way I feel, too."

"Just so we're clear, you said *ten million dollars*?" Blair was shaking her head and still processing, just like Ali had been.

"Yeah, now that's provided this real estate lady is right and knows her stuff. But she was recommended to me as the best."

"I can't breathe." Blair was waving her hands in front of her face.

"Honey, calm down. It's okay," Faye said.

"I just, what? That amount. It's what?"

Ali was concerned. She couldn't be right next to her baby sister if she passed out.

"Blair. Put your hands on your knees. You don't need to spiral. It's okay. We're the same three Kelly Sisters. This is just data we need to process. Take a breath."

"I get where she's coming from. This is like hitting the Powerball," Faye said.

"Breathe," Ali said.

Blair nodded. "I'm okay. I'm okay. I was just starting to get overwhelmed. I can barely manage Darla, much less a gazillion dollars."

Darla was Blair's cat, who seemingly ruled Blair's life and suffered from several skin conditions.

"You'll be able to hire Darla a butler if this is true," Faye pointed out.

"Okay," Blair said. "We can handle this. It's a strange problem, but a good problem."

"True that," Faye agreed. "If I become a millionaire, I am getting my chin hairs lasered off. Job one."

"What?"

"I'm so sick of plucking," Faye said.

Ali burst into a hearty laugh, and Blair did the same. Faye had helped them all see the absurdity of their current reality.

When they'd recovered, Ali said, "It's like it's all a fairytale that came after the weirdest stretch of my real life."

"Oh, gosh," Faye exclaimed. "We forgot to ask you! How are things moving with Ted?"

"No movement. My lawyer is waiting for him to get a lawyer. He wants my house, the house I worked so hard to make a home. So just how you'd expect."

"I'm sorry honey, men are the worst. Get this, Sawyer wants to leave college and take a gap year like he's a Kennedy or something."

"Oh, he had such great grades in high school. That's a shame," Ali said.

"Yeah, see, men, just not all right in the head.

Blair stayed quiet on the subject of men; they didn't know much about her current boyfriend.

Looking at her sisters surrounded by the ocean breeze gave Ali an idea.

"Why don't you both come down here? We aren't going to own it long. And it's got something so fun, so special, that it would be a shame not to experience it before we get rid of it."

Blair shook her head immediately.

"I can't, uh, Darla is under the weather."

"Oh, come on, just a weekend?"

"No, just let me know what we need to do to sell." They heard Blair's boyfriend call her name. "Coming! Gotta go." Blair clicked off the call abruptly.

"Well, goodbye then," Faye said and rolled her eyes. "You know, I like that idea of a visit. I'm going to hop on a plane, and I'll see you, what, on Friday, okay?"

"I love that idea."

"And we'll figure out how to be millionaires!!! Love you, Big Sissy!"

"Love you too!"

Ali was thrilled. Having Faye down here would be wonderful. She wouldn't have to decide everything herself.

And they'd get to experience a little of the magic of the Sea Turtle together before it floated out of their hands.

Twenty-Seven

FAYE

The numbers were more than she could believe. But Faye wasn't someone who counted her chickens before they hatched.

But she was someone with a bit of a temper. When she was mad, her co-workers at the plant said that was when she most reminded them of her dad. The Bruce Kelly Temper.

And it was her temper that got the best of her in the wine aisle of the Westgate Shopping Center Costco that day. She was browsing their selection of reds with an eye toward a glass to celebrate after her shift today. Becoming an almost millionaire seemed as good a time as any to have a glass of wine. But no matter how rich she got, she'd be darned if she would pay full price for anything!

"What do we have here!" she muttered to herself as she saw a shelf full of Black Tears Malbec.

Thirty-seven bucks was more than she'd normally spend, but Faye Kelly was about to become a fricking millionaire.

"Maybe I'll buy two!"

The Costco Wine Blog had it rated high, and it would be fifty bucks at a wine store, so it was a bargain. *Do rich people look for discounted wine? Well, this rich person will.* She wondered if rich people also perused the shorts and shirts on the clothing table? *What are you wearing? Kirkland.*

She giggled a bit to herself.

Faye continued down the aisle with the idea to peruse the lawn and garden offerings as well.

However, a middle-aged man and a much younger woman appeared at the end of her aisle. They were locked at the lips and hips. And they were in the dead center.

Faye didn't want to interrupt, but come on, canoodling in Costco? *How romantic.* She was mid-eye roll when the couple realized they were being rude and blocking the way with their display. They reluctantly stopped cuddling and looked at Faye.

When Faye recognized exactly who she'd caught canoodling, the Bruce Kelly Temper took over her brain. What's worse, it took over her mouth.

"Ted Harris, how embarrassing for you. Necking in the wine aisle at Costco with someone half your age? Yikes." It was one thing to hear about Ali's middle-aged husband and his girlfriend, it was something else to see it up close and disgustingly personal.

"Faye. Maybe lower your voice?"

"Well, it seems like you want everyone to know about your little girlfriend. Why else would your tongue be down her throat in broad daylight in front of the cheese sample lady?"

"You're being childish. We are both adults."

"Ah, so adults wear jeans that are way too tight, and is that hair dye you're doing now? So pathetic."

"I am in love with a person who appreciates me for the first time in my life. Something you'd know zero about. You're like a rabid dog the way you chase men away."

"Appreciates you?" Faye scoffed. "My sister is the best thing that ever happened to you. You're too arrogant to see that, aren't you, Professor?" Faye's tone was harsh, she knew, and she was glad. This man hurt her sister. And Ali Kelly Harris was the best wife, mother, and businesswoman in this town!

"I'm so glad to never have to sit at a Thanksgiving table or Christmas dinner ever again with you or the rest of the Kelly Sisters," Ted retorted. "Twenty-five years was enough. I've done my time with you uneducated hags!"

Ted always put his nose in the air because Faye and Bruce worked on the line. To him, blue-collar was an insult; to her, a point of pride. Ted saw her career and her dad's as one for the uneducated when, in fact, half of her co-workers had more training and education than he could imagine. And seriously, *done his time?*

"Well, you know Ted, that's something we agree on. And if you're so smart, you'd have played your cards right and you'd be a millionaire right along with Ali and us uneducated Kelly Sisters. That's right, our ship has come in. But you'd only know that if you were a good husband with half a brain, but alas, you're not."

"Millionaire?"

"That's right, it turns out we're about to multi-millionaires and you're out of luck, Professor. And no offense to you, uh, whatever your name is. But I'd run, don't walk, out of this little romance of yours. He didn't even make tenure until this year. How dumb must he be?"

Faye decided that was a decent enough parting shot. She angled her Costco cart around Ted and his girlfriend. She walked by with her head held high and did not look back.

Let Ted chew on the fact that not only had he lost Ali, but he'd also lost out on millions of dollars because he wanted to seem cool in front of his graduate assistant.

What a jerk.

Twenty-Eight

BELINDA
1984

It started with a phone call in the middle of the night. Joetta was almost impossible to understand. She cried, she slurred, and she yelled into the phone.

Belinda tried to calm her sister. How could she help if she didn't understand a word Joetta was saying.

Car crash. Arrested.

Bail.

Only later would Belinda know the true severity of what happened. During the midnight phone call, Belinda got this.

All three of Joetta's little girls had been in the car when Joetta crashed it. Belinda nearly threw up at the shock of the news. Baby Blair wasn't even one yet!

"Are they okay? Are the girls okay? Are they hurt?"

It was the only question and the worst question.

"I think they're okay. They won't let me out. They won't let me see."

Her sister clearly needed a lawyer. And bail money. Belinda didn't have a clue how to do any of that.

"Honey, I must tell Mom and Dad. I have no clue how to get you that money or a lawyer."

Cornwell Bennett knew lawyers, dozens of them. Belinda didn't mince words with her parents. She told them it was life or death. That Joetta was in jail and that she needed help. Belinda didn't flinch or equivocate. She demanded her parents take action to help. For the first time in her life, she stood up and told them how it was going to be.

And it worked. Her father did as she asked despite not having seen his daughter for almost a decade. When it was laid in front of him that he had to help, he helped. Belinda's heart will always remember that moment with her father.

And her mother. Well, their mother held her nose throughout. She watched and grimaced as her husband made phone calls.

From what Belinda gathered, even with their money and connections, Joetta would have to spend three nights in lock-up.

It was a weekend. They were doing everything they could from across the country, but it wasn't going to get Joetta out until Monday.

Over those same three days, Belinda booked a flight. She would be there for Joetta when she was arraigned. By 7 a.m. Monday morning, Cornwell Bennett's Tampa attorney had roused a Toledo, Ohio, attorney he knew. They conveniently had docks next to each other at the Tampa Yacht and Country Club.

The attorney was there, and so was Belinda, as Joetta faced a municipal court judge. Belinda had never been in a courthouse. It was scary, foreign, and overwhelming. Her poor sister had to be so afraid!

When the deputies brought Joetta out into the courtroom, Belinda gasped.

Her sister looked to be under one hundred pounds, and her skin was the color of paste. She had a gash on her forehead.

Belinda thought her sister should have had stitches, but instead, there was just a mess of gauze and medical tape.

Her pretty little sister looked like a waif. Or a ghost.

Joetta's lip quivered when she locked eyes with Belinda. She saw her eyes scan the room and lock to the back of the gallery.

Belinda turned to follow Joetta's gaze. There he was. Bruce Kelly's arms were crossed over his chest. His lips were in a thin line. There was no relief on his face at the sight of his wife, only disdain.

The judge spoke, and Joetta nodded. The attorney whispered to her what to say and where to sign. And then it was over. Joetta was released on bond and given a court date. As soon as Joetta was allowed, she flew into Belinda's arms. The sisters hugged, and the attorney explained the next steps. There was no waiting embrace from her husband. Bruce Kelly hung back, away, disconnected from the crisis that embroiled the family. Joetta tried to go to him. She reached out and put a hand on his.

"I'm so sorry. I'm so sorry. The girls."

Bruce picked Joetta's hands off him like they were contaminated. Their relationship had obviously been cold when Belinda had visited before, but since then, it had turned into something ugly. And Belinda knew she couldn't put that all on her brother-in-law.

Joetta had made a terrible mistake. And it was way worse than her headaches and a broken wine glass in the middle of the night.

"The girls are with my parents. You won't be seeing them right now. Maybe ever."

"What are you saying? Are they okay? Honey, it was an accident. It was a deer; it came out in the middle of the road and—"

He put a hand up to stop her explanation. "Do not come back to the house. You're a danger to my family. It is a shame you didn't die in that crash. At least then you'd be unable to do more damage."

Belinda stepped in. That was awful to say, to hear. Joetta was clearly sick and needed help! She would help. She would get her on her feet, and Bruce would see reason.

"Come on," Belinda said to Joetta. "Let's get you cleaned up. You two can talk about this when everyone's calmer." Though, to be honest, the man looked calm, scarily calm. Belinda had never been so frightened in her life of someone so calm.

"I just need to hug the girls; can't I just do that? They'll want to see me too. I'm sure they were so afraid?"

"They were. They won't be again."

That sounded more final than anything Belinda had ever heard. They won't be again...

Bruce Kelly turned and began to walk away. Joetta's demeanor became more and more like a panicked wild animal.

Who is this woman? Is this what she's become?

"You can't!" Joetta yelled. "They need me. I need to see them. I need to be sure they're okay. I need—"

"You need to shut up and maybe let your sister clean up your mess this time. We are no longer doing that."

Bruce walked away, shoulders square. He was a brick wall. He was impenetrable.

Belinda didn't know how to fix this. Her sister's life was a disaster, careening toward tragedy. *Thank God the girls are okay. Thank God.* Belinda clung to that one ray of hope. And then Joetta collapsed onto the sidewalk. Her waling turned into whimpering.

"Here, come on, I've got a car. Let's get into the car. I'm at the Sheraton, on Secor. We'll go there, get you a shower, and figure out what to do next. I'm sure after the dust settles, we'll get you over to the house. Things will be okay."

"No, they won't. He won't. He's like that. He said this was my last chance the last time and then this."

"What last time?" Belinda wondered what other calamities her sister had caused. While Bruce was cold and frightening, Belinda feared that Joetta had earned at least a portion of what was happening right now. How far down had she slid since Belinda had visited and witnessed her niece be the adult and her sister be the child?

"I don't have anywhere to go. I don't have clothes or my jewelry or anything."

"Like I said, let's go over to the hotel. Get you a shower. One problem at a time. It will all look better after you have a shower. Have a meal. Maybe we clean up that cut."

But nothing looked better. Only worse.

Belinda's only solution was to bring Joetta home without the girls. Belinda cleared it with the attorney, and he said as long as she was back for her court date, she could travel in the contiguous U.S.

Maybe with a little time and distance, her husband would see reason. He'd forgive his wife.

They stopped at a store called Jacobson's, and Belinda bought her sister underwear, a bra, and something to wear on the plane.

It was the only thing Belinda could think of to help.

Her heart was breaking for her sister. But worse, it was breaking for her three little nieces who had last seen their mother bleeding behind the steering wheel.

Get Joetta home, get her head looked at, get her maybe to Alcoholics Anonymous? This was rock bottom. Belinda hoped it was, anyway. *Wasn't that the turning point for people? When they had no further to fall, they finally stopped drinking?*

Belinda took charge, but inside, she was filled with doubt. But if she was going to get Joetta better, she needed to get her out of Toledo. In a few weeks, she'd be sober, healthier, a few good meals in her, rest. All these things would help Bruce see that he needed her and the girls needed her.

Joetta was a zombie. She didn't fight Belinda's plan and she didn't rage against her husband's edict not to see the girls.

She showered when Belinda told her to shower, she wore what Belinda laid out, she sipped coffee when it was in front of her, and she got on the plane.

Belinda didn't know this person. This person was so far away from the vibrant baby sister she grew up with that it terrified her.

She didn't say any of that to Joetta. Joetta was used to being dictated to these days. She was used to not taking charge of anything, it appeared.

Joetta slept the entire flight from Toledo to Tampa.

Belinda did not. Belinda silently rehearsed what she was going to tell their parents.

She had stuck up for Joetta to get the lawyer, and that was just the beginning. The era of Joetta being abroad was over. Joetta was coming home. And their parents were going to help. Even if it only meant opening a checkbook, not their hearts.

Twenty-Nine

ALI

She'd prepared a little send-off. Ali knew the Hafners and the Nobles were hitting the road at 9 a.m., so she made five "go bags" of coloring books and treats. She'd also printed out a couple of photos of the family frolicking on the beach that she'd snapped and put them in little frames. She made a note to check on getting custom frames with the Sea Turtle Resort logo on them.

No, Ali, bad Ali, that's not what someone who's going to SELL does.

It was hard to not plan improvements or stop her brain from coming up with hospitality ideas. That had been her career, and this place was tailor-made for her to do what she loved on a way more personal scale than Frogtown.

She found the Riveras back to work, doing their best to keep up. Jorge was supervising as Didi got to work on washing the linens for the next round of guests.

The booking calendar showed that they had two families again headed for the cottages, and Didi said they had four families booked for the next week, which was spring break for a lot of people.

"Unless?"

Didi knew that Patsy Gleaner had toured the resort.

"Look," Ali reassured her, "I know we're selling, but I wouldn't dream of ruining a family's hard-earned vacation."

"That makes me so relieved. The Fromer family has been here every year since the pandemic. We're so fond of them."

"Of course. But the cottages, are they all up to snuff? I need to do an inventory to be sure they're ready." Ali had stepped into managing the resort almost seamlessly. She realized she wanted to be sure the guests were well taken care of—in a place she didn't even know she owned until a few weeks ago!

"Have you considered staying?" Didi asked. "You're good at this! Look at you, making sure they all have treats." Didi pointed to the go bags Ali had made.

"Oh, I think it's a lovely life here, but no. It's not just me involved. My sisters are equal owners, and this is a lot of money to turn down."

"I understand, I do. But you know, everyone who stays here becomes a member of the family. It will be tough to see that end."

Didi looked a bit deflated at Ali's answer, but other than that wistful moment, she didn't push. It was clear that even if Ali hadn't come along to sell, Jorge and Didi were going to have to really retire soon. It was too much to manage at their age. They'd done enough.

By nine a.m., Ali stood in the parking lot to help see off the Hafners and Nobles. She'd earned hugs from the little ones and gratitude from the moms for all the things she'd done to make the place special.

The moms had become her new friends in the short time they were here. Didi was right about that.

"I really hope you don't sell," Kerry Hafner said.

"You too? How'd you hear?"

"It's Haven Beach gossip that you'll sell. If so, it will probably be our last trip down here. There's nothing this cute or affordable unless you book in July. But uh, July?"

She laughed. Ali figured the summer months would be a bear, weather-wise.

As she said goodbye to their guests, she was immediately caught in another hug.

An Uber had pulled in, and Faye had popped out. She was simultaneously waving goodbye and hello.

"Baby Sister!"

"Big Sister!"

The two embraced, and Ali was so happy to see her face. This was the longest she'd ever gone without seeing Faye. She realized her quick visit had turned into three weeks.

"Who were those families?"

"Well, we had two guests here in the cottages this week. There's only one in the hotel, and today is move-out day."

"You sound like you own the place."

"Ha, yeah, well?"

Ali helped Faye with her bag, and they strolled the little paths that made the Sea Turtle Resort look more like a village than a group of cottages.

"Oh my gosh, is this Yucca? And this might be Passiflora!" Ali didn't know what Faye was talking about, but she was running from plant to plant. "Passiflora, passion flowers, I cannot imagine what it would be like to grow in this zone all year."

"You're being generous. This place needs some serious land-scaping." Through Faye's eyes, though, Ali started to have a new appreciation for the overgrown foliage.

"Oh, for sure."

Ali watched Faye get distracted by the palm fronds that drooped low over the deck of the Mango.

"I'm going to put you here, second best view of the beach but best mattress."

"This is so cute; I can't stand it. Like I cannot stand it."

"Well, don't fall completely in love. The water pressure isn't great, and I'm pretty sure that four of the six light fixtures need replacing."

"Nitpicking, that's your attention to detail that we all, uh... love, that's it, love."

"Ha, ha."

"Seriously, what in the world? How did we not know this was ours? It's like Fantasy Island or something!"

"Dad, he knew. He was the one who packed up all that stuff of Mom's. He had secrets from us, and this was the biggest one."

"Let's have this conversation out there, yeah?" Faye's eyes were on the beach.

Just a few days prior, the water had pulled Ali's gaze out there in that same hypnotic way. She was glad to see she wasn't the only one affected by how stunning it was.

"Yeah, I've got snacks. Meet me out there after you get changed."

A short while later, Ali and Faye sat with their toes in the sand. Ali was so glad to be able to talk to Faye. Faye's reaction to this place was the same as Ali's. She watched her sister take a deep breath of the sea air.

"I'm so glad you're getting to see this, and when you meet Jorge and Didi, you'll fall in love with them, too."

"The two that let the pool turn green?"

"It's just bad luck. He had a hip thing. She seems like she's near 80. This is a lot to manage, I think."

"You seem to be doing just fine."

"You know, I love this kind of thing. It's sort of like the convention space. Still, instead of worked-up vendors jockeying for position and complaining about the sound system, I have been able to help families have a luxurious vacation on a reasonable budget."

"Um, what you did for Frogtown all those years—heck, for me and Blair too, for that matter? This is your gift, making magic for other people."

It was the same thing Ali had heard Henry say about Didi.

"I *did* turn it out when Dad took us to Cedar Point." It was true. Ali had done her best to be sure Blair and Faye had fun, and had Magical Moments, ala Disney, without actual Disney. Maybe Faye was right. She should have been a travel agent.

"You know, if we make all this dough the real estate agent says we're going to make, you could get a bed and breakfast in Northern Michigan or Irish Hills or something. That'd be a cool job."

"Ha, I've heard Irish Hills property is hard to come by these days. Dad wouldn't believe how his old summer lake is turning into the Hamptons of the Midwest."

"Right?"

"But yeah, that kind of money is potentially life-changing. I've been thinking a lot about life changing. Divorce, Dad gone, no job. It's been a month," Ali said. She had barely unpacked all the changes. She also hadn't looked forward.

What do I want to do—other than make sure the guests coming tomorrow have a lovely first Grand Finale?

"It seems sort of weird to sell a place like this and then buy another one, I guess. Oh my gosh, is that a shark fin?"

Ali looked out to the water. "No, school of dolphins. Look over there!"

Three more fins bobbed in and out, and it became clear that what they were seeing was play not searching for prey.

"Oh wow, just wow."

They sat in silence for a moment and let the breeze and the waves fill the space.

"I feel like my shoulders just released from my ears," Faye sighed, "and I didn't know I was scrunching them up."

"Yeah, there's a very chill vibe out on this beach." Ali remembered the wave of calm that had washed over her the first time she was here.

"Man, let's never leave."

"Yeah, easy to say, but uh, ten million bucks?" The number didn't seem real. What seemed real was breathing this air and feeling the sun on their legs.

Ali's phone buzzed and interrupted her moment of calm. "Oh, it's Barb Burns, that divorce attorney!"

She had alerted Barb that she was going to be formally separating from Ted but hadn't done anything about it yet. Time enough when she got back to Toledo to get into the divorce settlement. She figured she'd keep the house, Ted would get an apartment, he'd keep his car, and she'd keep her 401K.

"Barb Burns, here."

"Hi Barb, yes, how are you?"

Barb didn't mince words or answer how she was. "I needed to give you a heads up."

"What about?"

"Did you get an appraisal of the property in Florida?"

Ali had no idea why Barb would care or know about it. "Nothing formal, but it appears we're sitting on a decent-sized real estate investment."

"Well, I just got a document request for everything related to the Sea Turtle resort."

"From whom?"

"Ted. He wants a formal appraisal, and it appears he's going to claim half of whatever you get if you sell it."

"What? He doesn't even know about this place."

"Hiding assets isn't allowed in a divorce."

"I haven't filed yet, and I'm not hiding anything. I haven't even got this place on the market. How does he know any of this?"

"I don't know. But if you're sitting on a ten-million-dollar windfall, split three ways, make sure you know that you're going to be splitting your third by half with Ted. I'll email you the information I need."

"Okay." Ali's heart sank. *What was Ted thinking? Fighting over something he had no right to, something he shouldn't even know about, really?*

"Was that what I think it was?" Faye asked.

"Yeah, Ted's attorneys want half of my theoretical third of whatever we get for this place. How in the world does he know what we're sitting on here? And the gall to think he should have a piece of it!" Ali was livid. Ted had called a lawyer and decided to pick through her business, all the while sleeping with his teaching assistant.

Faye's face was red. And they hadn't been out long enough for sunburn. Faye got up, paced a few times, and then turned to Ali.

"Um, yeah...that's my fault. Oh my gosh, it's my fault! I rubbed his nose in it."

"What?"

ALI

"This is my fault. Totally my fault."

Faye was pacing up and down the little stretch of beach that had, up until a few minutes ago, been paradise.

Sunset was on the way, and today, Didi and Jorge had insisted they handle the Grand Finale. Faye and Ali were the only ones staying in the cottages, so it would likely be a smaller affair than the last few days had been.

Jorge and Didi had handled it for the last fifteen years. So why was Ali taking this on as her responsibility? But she was. She was worried Didi would get overheated or Jorge would try to carry too much.

Ugh. Focus on your own issues!

"It's just a shocker, the fact that he's the one that filed and that he's going after this place. Like, I might be the one who has to pay alimony? Is that even possible?"

"That cheater? I mean, that's what set me off. He was cuddling with this co-ed at Costco, and I just blurted it all out. You didn't cheat, you shouldn't have to pay."

"Well, that's not how it works. We would have had to split things, and since he made more and was the one at fault, I was likely going to get support. I mean, I don't want that, but I did quit my own college to work when he was in school." Ali had started booking the banquet at the Sheraton Hotel and then eventually moved into the convention space. She had never finished her degree.

"And now he wants this place?"

"The lawyer said my third split in two, but I mean, it's not like we knew we had this place. So—"

"—I am *livid*. He shouldn't get a dime from you!"

Slowly, the usual audience for the Grand Finale trickled onto the beach. Erica from the coffee shop greeted Didi and Jorge, and then Ali waved her over to meet Faye.

"You look like you need this more than me," Erica said, handing Faye a glass.

"I like her already," Faye quipped to Ali and gulped it down.

"I'm thinking something is going on, what's happening?"

Faye looked to Ali, and Ali nodded. She hadn't spoken much about her marital situation. But she also wasn't trying to hide anything. She actually needed advice and counsel right now. She'd found Erica to be a cool head with good insights. She listened as Faye summarized Ali's current disaster of a personal life.

"Her soon-to-be ex-husband, after ruining the marriage, wants to ruin her future by getting his hooks into this place after it's liquidated or whatever."

Ali winced at the term liquidated. She hated the idea.

"Oh, ex," Erica replied, "that clears that up, Henry was asking."

Faye looked at Ali, who shrugged. *Why would he be asking?*

"Whoa, who's tall, pepper, and handsome over there?"

Faye had spotted Henry.

Ali was uncomfortable with all the talk of her handsome new friend, so she tried to change the tone.

"Faye, this is Henry Hawkins. He owns the Seashell Shack; we'll have to go over tomorrow for lunch."

"Nice to meet you."

He had a good smile; Ali couldn't deny that. Faye looked at Ali and Henry a few times. Ali gave her little sister the stink eye to cool it with whatever mischief she was thinking.

Ali wasn't feeling flirty or playful. She was feeling mad. That was it. She was mad as heck that Ted would have the gall to serve her divorce papers and make demands.

"Ali's soon-to-be ex just dropped a bomb," Erica said.

"Ah, I'm sorry. Divorce is a terrible process. I can attest."

"Yeah, Sherry raked this one over the coals," Erica explained. "Thank goodness you lost, though, or you wouldn't be here."

"I am glad for that every day. Sometimes, a loss turns into a win. If that's any consolation."

"Well, Ted, her soon-to-be ex, wants the proceeds of the sale of the Sea Turtle thanks to me opening my big mouth."

"It's not your fault. Well, maybe the timing is your fault," Ali said and took a sip of the wine.

"I can't help thinking the solution is obvious," Erica said.

"What's that?" Ali asked.

"Don't sell this place. No sale, no major cash influx."

Ali looked at Faye. "It's not just about me. I'm one of three owners. My sisters are equal partners."

Faye started hopping around like she was on fire. "No, she's right! That's it. We're not selling. You're going to run this place. And Ted can take half of the third of your green pool and suck it with a straw!"

Henry and Erica laughed.

"Oh, I like her already," Erica said.

Ali loved the idea of running this place. She had been fantasizing about it from almost the first moment she'd stepped on the beach. She imagined waking up each morning here, taking a walk, having coffee on the deck, and, more than anything else, making wonderful memories for guests here.

But it was a fantasy. She knew that.

"Faye, I am not a resort manager."

"You're great at it. The Hafners and Nobles were going on and on at The Shack the other day about how you'd made their stay magical," Henry said.

"I did not." She deflected the compliment, but it gave her a warm feeling inside.

"Stop," Faye said. "You're always doing that. She ran the biggest convention center in Lucas County. For a decade. This place is tiny by comparison."

"It's not the same thing."

"It is, too. You handle the details and make people happy. Period. Why not do it here?"

Ali's heart beat a little faster. *Why not do it here?*

"It's crazy."

"Both of us started again, right here, with my restaurant and her bakery," Henry pointed out.

"Maybe it's not called Haven Beach by accident," Faye offered.

"No, this is very sweet of you all, but this isn't my life."

"It sure looks like your life," Erica said.

"And think about how mad Ted would be," Faye added. "Oh, I need to be there when he finds out."

Ali shook her head; she wasn't going to stand in the way of her sisters and a huge cash windfall. No matter how much it started to feel like a dream come true.

"Holy Toledo," Faye said as the focus shifted from their conversation to the fireball in the sky, sinking and dazzling with every inch it fell into the blue water.

The sun was setting over the water, a glowing orange ball

sliding down into a creamy salmon sky with the bluest water to land in.

"Grand Finale doesn't disappoint," Henry said.

"No, it never does," Ali replied.

"Man, I may never leave either," Faye said, and they sipped their wine and watched the greatest show on Earth.

Thirty-One

ALI

They'd watched the sunset and finished the bottle of wine, and Faye had made fast friends with the locals that Ali had to admit were already like family to her now.

Ali had moved back into the Key Lime but couldn't sleep.

The suggestion that she upend her life and stay here, to try to run this place, kept rolling around in her mind. It was ludicrous. *Wasn't it?*

She longed to ask Ted his opinion. That was the irony of it. Usually, he would be her sounding board in this kind of situation.

When making any major life decision, she would talk with Ted. Change jobs. Have another baby. Refinance the house. Call hospice for Dad. Ted had been the person who helped her make those decisions.

Ted was her husband. They'd had their ups and downs. But she'd loved him. Did she still? He was a good dad. He instilled a love of reading in both kids. He supported Tye on the soccer field and Katie when she played softball. He'd cheered just as loud as Ali did at every game. He was there for the kids. And that alone made her grateful to him. They shared Tye and Katie, and it was a bond that would never go away. *Or would it?*

Ted was there for her, too, at the big moments. He'd encouraged her to move from the hotel job to the convention center and to ask for more responsibility. He knew she could handle it.

"You're the smartest one in the building with the most organizational skills. They're not using you to your potential," he'd said. She'd glowed then when he'd complimented her.

But somewhere along the line, it had gone wrong. Was it her fault that he'd found someone else? Or were they just a cliché? He was a man in his midlife, so of course he was afraid he was getting old. And there were always young women around him.

Always young women around him.

She blinked. Always young women around him. This trip down marriage memory lane unlocked something in her memory. Something she'd either forgotten about or repressed!

Five years prior, they'd had a terrible situation. Ted's student... Amber Covell, that was her name. She'd started stalking Ali. She'd show up at Ali's work, she would call on the phone and hang up, and eventually, Ali had to block the girl's phone number.

Ted had said that Amber was mentally unstable and just was fixated on their family. Ted had said she was jealous of Ali. Ali wondered now, what was the source of that jealousy?

It was like a missing piece of the puzzle of their lives just clicked into place.

Ali opened her phone settings and clicked on Call Blocking and Identification. She had only blocked one or two spam numbers in her life. She scrolled down.

There it was. A 419-area-code. Amber.

It was 10 p.m., not too late, but who cared. Ali had gone down a rabbit hole, and she wasn't going to let it go. She couldn't.

She dialed the number.

Three rings and then a voice: "Hello."

"Amber, hello. This is Ali Harris. I don't know if you remember me."

"Hello. Yes. I remember you. Hard not to remember."

Ali didn't really know what she was talking about. This was silly. This girl was unbalanced, and Ali was stirring up old issues on a hunch.

"I'm calling because I need to know something. And it's okay if you want to hang up, but I'm trying to figure some things out."

"Okay. Go on."

"Ted told me you were obsessed with him, stalking him, and that you just sort of had a crush that was one-sided."

"Interesting story. But yeah, no."

"You didn't have a crush on him?"

"Mrs. Harris, Ali. Do you want me to answer with the truth? Because you won't like it. I've moved passed this, and I don't want to cause pain."

"I called because I want the truth. You are doing me a favor."

Amber paused. The tension had Ali feeling like a rubber band stretched to snapping.

And then Amber spoke softly, calmly. As though she was walking on eggshells. "I slept with your husband back then. I was twenty, mind you, so clearly very stupid."

Ali felt like a deer in the headlights as she listened to Amber. "So, you two had a fling," Ali said.

"Yes, and then I found out he was also sleeping with his grad assistant. I walked in on them during office hours."

"Ted was cheating on me with his grad assistant and then cheating on the grad assistant with you?"

"Yeah, real great guy."

Ali was horrified. This was more than just a midlife crisis. This was a pattern. One she'd ignored or didn't see or didn't want to see.

"I just never knew. I never suspected. I'm so sorry."

"You've got nothing to be sorry for. He's a real jerk. And I'm sorry, I was calling you back then to tell you. To blow up your life or save you. I don't know. I'm still in therapy on some of this. He wasn't the first older boyfriend or the last."

"Ah." Ali was at a loss for words. *What do I say to this? How can I reconcile that this was Ted's pattern, not a one-off?*

"You're not still with that guy, are you?" Amber asked.

"No, no, I'm not. We're recently, uh, separated."

"Good, stay separated. That's my advice."

"Yeah, yeah. And I'm sorry to bother you or dredge things up. I just needed some clarity."

"Good luck with that."

"Thank you. Take care of yourself."

"You too, Mrs. Harris, you too."

The call ended. Ali's world had shifted again. What had been confused was now clear.

She didn't need Ted's career advice. She didn't need Ted. What she needed was to do what she wanted, what her heart was telling her to do.

And she was darn sure she didn't want Ted to have one dime from the Sea Turtle Resort, now or ever.

Thirty-Two

FAYE

Faye's arms were open for Ali this time as opposed to the other way around.

"I'm such a fool. I missed it. All these years, I missed it."

Faye had opened her cottage door to an Ali in pieces. Faye had never seen Ali break down. She'd been so stoic, from the death of their father to the discovery of Ted and his grad assistant, and even when her kids went to college.

But now, she was in pieces.

Ali cried. Faye listened, and she got to comfort her big sister. Faye and Blair had relied on Ali as a stand-in for their mother. It was easy to forget that Ali was less than two years older than Faye. Blair, the baby, was so much younger. Their baby doll. But Ali was a baby, too, when all that happened.

"We all missed it. He was good at pulling the wool over everyone's eyes. I mean, if Dad had suspected, he'd have punched his lights out."

Ali sniffled and pressed a tissue to her nose. Faye gave her space.

Faye wanted Ali to feel safe, she wanted her to know she was allowed to cry, allowed to feel what she felt. Blair knew her sister had bottled so much, for so long.

Ali sat on the little rattan lounge in the vintage cottage. There were obvious things to fix around her update, but there was also something so calming. The minute you walked from the parking lot to the property of the Sea Turtle Resort, you felt differently about the life you left.

Was that magic? Or was it the sea air?

"I need to stay here. Or at least, stay away. I don't want to see Ted. I don't want to step into that house. I just don't. Is this selfish of me?"

"You don't have to. But what do you want to do next? Just chill? Because that's allowed, too. You don't always have to have a plan or a goal. And no, you're the least selfish person I know."

"It's just that I feel better with a plan and a goal. I just need a different one than what I'd been working toward all these years."

"You want to make a go of this place, don't you? I see it in you. Feel it. Saw it with the way those families hugged your neck when they left. You're made to be here, or it was made for you."

Ali nodded. She was pulling herself back together. Faye watched Ali think, calm her breathing, and focus.

This was her big sister. The one who had it under control. Control was returning after her dam had burst.

"It's the least practical thing I could do—*we* could do—to hang on to this place and not cash in."

"Here's something I've been learning; you need to learn it too. It's not the money. It's the purpose. We all need a purpose, something that makes us want to get out of bed in the morning. You know? When our kids are little, it's easy. You're doing it for them. Sometimes, it's the job you love and the people you work with. But sometimes, it all seems to vanish. The reason I got out of bed and headed to the plant was to, you know, show Dad, show everyone how tough I was. That isn't the same anymore. I was trying to prove something to everyone. But what for?"

"Yeah, I get it, but several million bucks at the flick of a pen would give you time to buy a new purpose."

Faye laughed. That was true. "But why search when you have a purpose right here?"

"I can't take this away from you or Blair."

"You have given us way more than we could ever repay. And I expect you to make this work. We'll have a nice source of income. And a gorgeous place on the water to visit. I don't see a problem. Oh, and we'll drive Ted absolutely bat crap crazy. See? That's a win-win!"

Ali laughed. Good: laughter through tears was a great emotion, to paraphrase Dolly Parton in *Steel Magnolias*.

"You know, we can always change our minds."

"Right, give it a go for what, a season or two? If it isn't what you want, we bail. But before that, you need to settle."

"Settle?"

"Settle with Ted, give him the house."

That idea put a little bit of panic in Ali's eyes.

"I know. I know. You made that house. But look, here's how you shut him up. He gets the house. You get your little inheritance from Dad to live on, and we bet on our future with this place."

Ali nodded in agreement. She stood up and started to walk back and forth in the little cottage. Faye could see the wheels turning in her sister's brain.

"Right, okay, yes, I need to talk to my lawyer, Ted needs to sign off. And he needs to know I'm not kidding around."

"Ted's hooks have to be out of this place, so you don't have him influencing you or profiting from you. However it shakes out."

Ali stopped and looked at Faye. "What about Blair? She needs to be okay with this."

Faye stood up and put her hands on Ali's shoulders.

"Leave Blair to me. I'll get her to sign off. We all three own the place, but you're the boss. She knows that. And she owes you the life she had, just like I do. I can't imagine a better mom than you. And neither can Blair."

Ali sucked in a ragged breath at those words.

"I could never be Mom," she whispered.

"You never needed to be; you were better. I know," Faye said.

The two sisters hugged it out. Faye didn't remember much, but she did remember a mother who had "headaches" and forgot things and a big sister who never did. Not once.

Faye would make a phone call in the morning to get Blair on board. She wasn't sure how hard that would be. But it didn't matter. The two little sisters were doing this for their big sister.

Period.

And they were doing this to Ted. Which was equally as motivating.

Once Ali had made up her mind to stay, it was hard not to love watching her plan.

"We need the pool fixed first, and then, what about mid-century modern for the Inn, like lean into it? We could create such a lovely experience here that won't break the bank. I just really love the idea of keeping part of the beach, this place, for people like us who aren't billionaires. You know?"

Ali was on fire, and Faye found joy in helping to make that happen.

Now, to handle Blair, and her life back in Toledo.

Her time in Sea Turtle was amazing, but her life wasn't on Haven Beach. It was back up north.

Thirty-Three

ALI

The Mangrove County offices were in a pink stucco building.

Pink. Okay then.

Ali thought back to her hometown. Toledo had a reputation as a rust belt town. As something less than, maybe, even the punchline to a joke. But that was wrong. Toledo was vibrant and beautiful, and its downtown along the waterfront sparkled. She was proud to change minds on The Glass City every time she booked an event for Frogtown.

Her own neighborhood celebrated the architecture of a bygone era. She was used to older neighborhoods and buildings sitting side by side with newer ones. Toledo was like that.

Ali realized that she'd been up and down the beach in several towns, and it was mostly new. She didn't see the old and historic. Was it hurricanes? Or was it just that this part of Florida wasn't settled until later? She wondered. The good news was she also didn't see gray slush on the sidewalk, so there was that.

This building, with its pink stucco, couldn't be more of a

contrast to county offices in Toledo. But inside, well, inside, it couldn't be more the same. Counters, cubicles, and the maze of slow-moving red tape. That was also part of her job in Toledo, navigating it to get the approvals she needed to get her things done.

Ali visited a clerk's window and made her inquiry.

"Hello, I'm looking for the history of a property on Gulf Boulevard."

The clerk, a curvy woman with a floral blouse and the ability to raise a single eyebrow at Ali, removed her readers. They were draped around her neck on a crystal chain. "Address?"

"13 Gulfside Way. It would have been a real estate transfer in the 1980s."

"Uh, good luck. None of those are digitized. You're going to need to go to room 205, that's down the hall. Let me write down the cabinet."

"The cabinet??"

"Yeah, anything prior to my time here, so 1980, they're in the cabinets in 205. There's a microfiche reader. Instructions are on the side."

"Any advice on how to find it?"

"Well, take your best guess at the year and find that cabinet, then address by address."

"Oh, okay, wow."

"Yeah, so much easier to Google, ha. But then I'd be out of a job, right?"

"Yes, uh, well, that would be bad, uh, no?"

The woman rolled her eyes at Ali.

"Don't worry, I'm joking."

The woman pointed her in the right direction and Ali let her presumably get lost in paperwork hell.

Ali had done some research here and there for her job with the convention center. They'd pulled permits for expansion and dealt with building regulations and liquor licenses, and she felt confident she'd find something. Even if she didn't know exactly where to look here.

Ali wound up in a room full of file cabinets and walked by the early 2000s, past the 1990s, and finally found cabinets labeled with 1980 on the front.

She narrowed it down to 1984 and then through the streets, listed alphabetically. Gulf had half a file cabinet and three drawers. She figured that owed to the fact it was the longest street on Haven Beach. She made her way through the addresses, and after only fifteen minutes in the records room, she found the file cabinet she hoped had answers.

In 1984, the Sea Turtle Resort was given over to her and her sisters. They were little then. Only children.

Why? Who would give three little girls this property? Was it an investment? How in the world did it come to be?

She looked at her phone. Back in Toledo, she'd taken a picture of the deed. There should be an exact duplicate in here.

They were arranged by street, and then by date. Ali pulled the microfiche reel out and loaded it into the machine.

This had to be it!

She hoped this was right. A surprising mix of emotions tumbled around in her chest. She didn't know why she was nervous, but solving a mystery where you were the mystery probably explained it.

The machine was easy to work, so Ali cranked the handle to advance the film.

She read one deed transfer after another, addresses she didn't recognize, until there it was:

13 Gulfside Way.

She read the description of the property. Six single-family cottages, a swimming pool, and an office structure. This was it.

It was doing business as the Sea Turtle Resort, even back then. She had to imagine not many places had retained their old names or structures. The state had expanded so much. At that point,

Epcot at Disney World was brand new. The tourist machine of the state was in full swing, but nothing like it would become.

There was a copy of the deed she'd found. She and her sisters were listed as the owners. And then she flipped back one more document.

The deed was transferred from Joetta Bennett to Ali, Faye, and Blair.

Ali audibly gasped.

Joetta Bennett was her mother, it had to be. Their father said her maiden name was Joetta Bowles. But not once had she ever seen a thing related to that name. *Why did he lie about her name?* But at least now Ali knew why there was no trace of Joetta Bowles, other than in their own home. Joetta Bowles didn't really exist. Joetta *Bennett* did and at one point she'd owned the Sea Turtle and beautiful gowns and jewels.

Joetta Bennett was her mother.

And when her mother died, she'd given the Sea Turtle to her daughters.

Ali shook with the realization that even though their mother had been gone all this time, she'd given them a gift.

Was there a will? Did it come to us that way?

Ali made notes with her questions.

But the main mystery was solved.

Their mother—their vulnerable, beautiful, tragic mother—wasn't as destitute as they thought. The things they'd found since their dad died had only served to make their mother more mysterious. She'd owned jewelry and designer clothes and now Ali saw her mother had owned real estate in Florida before she died. And before she died, she'd signed it over to her three children.

Ali felt a little dizzy. This upended what she knew about her mom. *And why in the world had their father never said anything?*

This could have been a way to pay for college or, at the very least, a place to visit on vacation. This would have been some small way to know their mother. Bruce Kelly had cut off all avenues of memory that his daughters could have pursued. She remembered his deathbed apology. *Was this it? Was this what he regretted? Keeping this secret?*

"It had to be done. Cut off. The only way."

He'd admitted it. That was what he was saying. Bruce Kelly, in his final breaths, had apologized for cutting them off from the memory of their mother. But why was it the only way? Why did he need to be sure they didn't know her memory. Or where she came from? Their mother had to be from Florida. This property had to mean she was from here.

The questions Ali had for her mother would never be answered. She'd resigned herself to that a long time ago. But with a harsh slap in the face, she realized she couldn't ask her father now either.

She'd lived a life without her mother. This was a familiar injury that she'd been able to close off. The scar had almost faded. Or so she thought.

But not being able to take Bruce Kelly to task over this, not being able to call him or talk to him, that was still so fresh. She could still hear his voice in her head.

Ali had long ago forgotten what her mother sounded like.

Bruce Kelly knew their mother left this resort to them and he'd never said a word. Never let his daughters know more about their mom. The seashells they'd found…She'd probably collected them from this place, this beach that seemed to call her home.

These revelations knocked the wind out of Ali. They upended her in a way that she didn't know how to fix. How did the world turn right side up after learning you knew nothing about something so important about your own life, your own family?

Ali took a breath. She had to calm herself, and deal in the present and in the reality of what she could do now, what she could know.

How did her mom come into this property? How did a young woman in her twenties own a resort to leave to her children?

Joetta Kelly was Joetta Bennett. And Joetta Bennett was a young woman with means. *How did she wind up a mother of three with nothing?*

Ali moved through the documents.

There were no more records in that year.

There were no more records of the Sea Turtle. At least that she could find. Ali had been warned that water damage from a long-ago storm had washed away records from the first thirty years of Mangrove County, that was well before everything was backed up on computers.

But one thing was clear. Her mother had given the Sea Turtle to them. And her father had hidden it away.

Why?

Her father's deathbed words echoed in her mind.

Thirty-Four

BELINDA
1984

Joetta was broken in body and mind. No matter how many times the two sisters tried to reason with Bruce Kelly, the pleas met with silence.

Eventually, Bruce answered one of Belinda's calls.

"I am sure that she won't understand. She's too addled to understand anything. But I will not let her near my girls. You can convey that to her. We aren't at the house. And won't be for some time."

Belinda's only hope was that Bruce would calm down, that he just needed time. She'd take care of Joetta. Get her healthier, and then when they went back to Toledo for the court date, Bruce would see reason, and Joetta would see the girls. This had to be true.

Joetta was in awe of Belinda's life. Belinda liked her life, but it didn't seem awe-inspiring by any stretch.

"You have your own apartment?" Joetta was amazed that Belinda didn't live in the big house with their parents anymore.

"I mean, it's not fancy or anything, but my salary at the country club is good, enough to pay for this place and for cute outfits."

Belinda grabbed a few clothes for Joetta to wear. Joetta was smaller, but the smock dresses would work.

"How is Banks?"

"Banks is good. He's a good boss. Way better than his dad was." Banks Armstrong had inherited the club from his father. And while he was their age, he had matured into a good person, one who had never stopped asking Belinda how Joetta was.

Belinda made it her mission to nurse Joetta back to something resembling the baby sister who'd left Florida in a hurry with a star-struck idea of love and life. Joetta's life had become all too real, all too fast.

Belinda made sure that Joetta slept; she was there when Joetta cried, and she was relieved when her sister slept again. This was a reset. That was what was needed, a do-over for her sister's life.

Joetta didn't drink at all since she'd walked out of the court-room. That was new.

After a few days, she looked more like herself. Gorgeously so. Joetta's blue eyes were free of bloodshot red. She seemed clearer each day she spent in Florida. Her pale skin began to get a little glow as Belinda encouraged her to sit by the apartment complex pool.

After a week of rest and care, Joetta said she felt and looked good enough to want to go to lunch at the club. Joetta, looking beautiful and refreshed and so thin you'd think she was a movie star, turned heads when they walked into brunch at the Armstrong.

The sisters enjoyed the brunch, with only a few staffers coming over now and then to ask Belinda this question about a day off or that request to leave early.

"You're so important," Joetta said.

Belinda wasn't necessarily important, but she did love her job here. She loved making the Armstrong better, taking care of guests, and knowing the answers to the questions she was asked. It gave her a sense of purpose and accomplishment.

It was something that Joetta didn't seem to have, confidence. Where had that gone? Did it evaporate when you became a mother? Was it because of Bruce? Or was it that accident? They'd avoided talking about what could have happened. That, really, Joetta was lucky. Her girls were alive.

Now, though, Joetta was feeling strong enough to bring it up.

"I called him, got through this time." *That was good. Bruce had answered her call!*

"And?"

"He said he was changing the phone number. I want to talk to the girls, but, well, that's a no-go. He just doesn't know that I'm sober. That I'm never going to drink again. Maybe when I show him that, he'll see reason."

"You can't drink ever again; you have a real problem."

"I know. And, well, I'm sorry. I'm sorry you had to clean up this mess with me. I'm sorry that my girls—" She stopped and put her hand up to her mouth. There was a lot of sorry, too much sorry to cover in one brunch.

"You don't need to apologize to me. I'm your sister. I'm always going to be here for you."

"And I'm going to go to those AAA meetings, I am. That's the next step. The judge will see that, too."

"AA."

"That's what I said."

Belinda laughed with her sister over the number of As she needed to manage. Joetta took a drink from the little juice glass filled with freshly squeezed Florida oranges. Nothing tasted this good, Belinda knew.

"The trouble was, I was a teenage mother in a town with no

one I knew, with a husband who, well, I didn't have what he needed in a wife. Cooking, cleaning, taking care of babies, I was not so good at it. I liked to decorate and shop. You saw that."

"I did. You'd made the house lovely with your thrifted magic!"

"He didn't give me a dime to spend. Do you know that? Not a penny on anything that wasn't cold cuts or white bread." She shuddered like that was a distant memory. Maybe it was when you were sitting in the sunroom annex of The Armstrong Dining Room.

When Belinda's boss and friend, Banks Armstrong, walked into the room, the connection between Joetta and Banks was immediate.

Belinda almost felt like a fifth wheel at the table, and she'd been there first.

Belinda saw Joetta move her hands that were sitting on her lap. When she offered her right hand to greet Banks, Joetta noticed the left one, on the napkin, was free of jewelry.

Joetta had slipped her wedding ring off.

Joetta's million-dollar smile belied the dime store life she'd just been kicked out of.

And Banks was in love. He had waited all this time for Joetta. Belinda didn't know how she felt about realizing that.

What was happening here?

Belinda watched in awe and took her baby sister's lead. Joetta wanted to be her old self for a moment. *Was that so wrong?* Belinda decided it was not.

"The club looks amazing! I love the improvements you've made."

"I've got a lot of help. Your sister here, top of the list of people who know how to treat guests."

"Ha, well, Walter Shwartz retired. That was a big improvement." Belinda was going to elaborate on how Walter, the old manager, had made life a living hell for everyone at the Armstrong. Still, she might as well have been on a different planet. Banks Armstrong was locked on Joetta like a tractor beam.

"You look beautiful. Life has been treating you well?"

Here it was. What was Joetta going to tell Banks about her life, and how it all had been treating her?

"I'm wonderful. Life's been a whirlwind. I can't believe I've been away so long! Traveling and adventure, you know."

Belinda watched as her sister became a different person. She wasn't the downtrodden housewife with no self-esteem and not enough coupons to buy groceries. Or the contrite alcoholic who'd just lost it all.

She was Joetta Bennett of the Florida Bennetts. Beloved and most beautiful daughter, heir, and apparently world traveler.

Banks Armstrong didn't care which version of Joetta he was talking to; he was clearly smitten by whatever yarn she decided to spin.

And spin, she did. Over the next few days, Banks called. Banks stopped by. Banks seemed to believe whatever Joetta told him.

Belinda was worried anew about what this all meant.

Almost two weeks went by.

Bruce continued to refuse her calls. But their parents opened their doors to the prodigal daughter. It was tense. Awkward. And also a relief. Joetta was home, and it appeared she had no additional baggage to explain.

The lie that she told Banks, she told to them. She had no children with her, so there must be no children. Belinda was a bystander as this fiction in their family solidified into fact.

Nothing bad happened if you didn't talk about it.

Joetta swung from happiness and almost glee when Banks would send a car or flowers or call on the phone, to despair.

One moment, she was leading Banks around on a string, and the next, she was hanging by a thread with Bruce. Belinda worried that her sister's sober life, her desire to put things right, was precarious.

Joetta cried to Belinda after every call.

"I just want to see my girls. Why won't he let me see my girls?"

It was hard to understand. Joetta was desperate to see her daughters but also equally as desperate to make a good impression on Banks. It's as if the two worlds were completely separate, and she was two different people in them.

Belinda listened to her beg Bruce, tempt him, and offer ideas to him.

"What if you move down here, Bruce, with the girls? They would love it. You could get a proper fishing boat?"

"What if I just visit for a few days so they know I'm better?"

Every phone call ended with Bruce hanging up.

If Joetta wanted to bring the girls, Belinda knew they had the perfect place!

Belinda made a suggestion.

"You know, we both have that resort property. Grandfather put it in my name. Mother was annoyed, but Daddy said it could be my nest egg since no one seems to be breaking down the door to marry me."

It was true Belinda didn't have a boyfriend, but she didn't want a boyfriend. And Daddy just thought he was being funny, not hurtful.

"Mother and Daddy say it's gauche. They were annoyed I got it in the will, but in the end, they didn't want it anyway. You know we've both always loved it so."

"I used to think about it a lot when it was cold in Toledo. It gets really cold. Do you manage the Sea Turtle *and* the Armstrong?"

"No, I have a management company dealing with it; maintenance and bookings. But what if I put it all in your name, and you and Bruce start fresh there?"

Belinda was grasping at straws, she knew, but maybe that was the issue. Maybe if Bruce Kelly had something in his name he could call his own, but something Joetta also contributed to, they'd find a new way forward. They could live here with the girls and start fresh. It sounded so perfect to Belinda. Bruce had to see it!

Joetta liked the idea, too.

She tried again to get through to her husband with this fresh plan.

But Bruce Kelly had stopped hanging up and started just not even answering.

Belinda didn't understand how Bruce could pass this up. *What was that man thinking?* Surely, he had to be able to forgive the mother of his children. Joetta was getting stronger every day. She was eating well, and she'd put a few pounds on the skeletal frame. Health looked possible for her.

They were at an impasse, Bruce and Joetta. And Belinda had taken her best shot at helping fix things.

Belinda had a peaceful life that she enjoyed. Her sister's reentry into her day-to-day had made it hard for her to handle her own responsibilities. This had to end.

The PGA Senior Invitational Golf Tournament was coming into town in a month, and she had a million details to sort out to be sure it was flawlessly executed. The tournament would be on TV, so the club had to be flawless. Belinda needed to tend to her own life now.

She'd gone into her office at The Armstrong determined to focus on doing just that.

Joetta was eating lunch with Banks, so both her boss and her sister were out of her hair. She had to get some work done.

Shortly after noon, her desk phone rang. She expected it was the pastry chef complaining about the order of key limes or maybe the laundry concerned they had too much to do with not enough dryer capacity. It was always something.

"Is this Belinda Bennett?"

"It is." She recognized the voice. Cold. Hard. And no emotion.

"Bruce? Is that you? Joetta has been trying and trying to get a hold of you. How are the girls?"

"It is. I've received a dozen mentally unstable messages from your sister."

Her sister? His wife! Belinda would tell Bruce about the resort. She'd sell the idea to Bruce even if Joetta couldn't.

"She is so sorry, so worried about the girls. She has a place here for all of you. The girls would love it. Did she tell you? You could start fresh. It's a resort with great rental income. On the beach. No blizzards!" Belinda knew she was sounding rather mentally unstable herself, rattling off a life plan for this man who had a life already.

"A divorce proceeding is beginning. I've told the girls their mother is gone."

Belinda's heart dropped to her stomach. She felt like she might be sick. "Gone?"

"You only know the end. You do not know what we've lived through. What they've lived through. I will no longer allow her to endanger my girls. And if she continues, I'll call your little society page and let them know how little Miss Joetta Bennett of the Florida Bennetts is a lush who nearly killed her entire family. How does that sound? Maybe I'll let them know when her court date is so they can get a good picture for the papers there."

"Bruce, that's not her. She has changed. Don't do this. She loves the girls. I love the girls!"

"If you love these girls, you'll want them to have a stable life without the mess that is your sister."

"Bruce, please, you can't deny them their mother."

"As far as they know, their mother is dead. You got it? And if you don't tell her to back off, I'll ruin her life there, just as sure as she almost ruined their lives here."

Belinda swallowed, again feeling the urge to be sick. She couldn't see a way forward. Whatever new life Joetta had could be destroyed by the news she'd crashed her car with her sweet girls inside. There'd be no future for Joetta here.

Belinda answered Bruce. "Okay." She agreed to his terms. No more contact. He'd keep his mouth shut, and she'd stay away from their girls. Belinda felt tears streaming down her eyes.

Ali! Faye! Baby Blair!

"I'm changing our numbers. Don't make me have to uproot the girls and move. I've already got a restraining order. Got it?" A restraining order. Did that mean Joetta would be breaking the law if she was near her own children? The idea was horrifying. But she understood now, after talking to Bruce. He truly believed he was protecting them. That this was the best way. Belinda worried, in her darkest places, that Bruce was right.

"Yes."

"Good, tell your sister. And leave us alone."

The line went dead.

Hours later, after her shift was over, Belinda and Joetta got in her car and drove out to Haven Beach. They had to talk, and Belinda didn't want Banks to interrupt. Joetta needed honesty, to get it, and give it.

Joetta listened, wide-eyed, to all that Belinda told her.

"He truly hates me. And the girls probably do, too."

"No. Never."

"You don't know. I was a terrible mother, what I can remember of it." Joetta put her head in her hands.

They sat together, side-by-side, on the beach blanket. The cottages were all booked, and families ran in and out of the surf as the sun went down.

"I've always loved this place so much," Belinda said. She didn't know what to say to her sister.

"I met Bruce right here."

And it was true. They'd spent so many summers right here, getting away from the stuffiness of the beach house and their parents.

"Maybe a cooling-off period is all you need; Bruce will calm down. He'll change his mind." Belinda had wanted to be honest but she found herself trying to find a silver lining for her beloved sister.

"No. No, he won't. And he shouldn't. He is a good dad. He loves the girls."

"You love the girls."

"I do. But I'm no good for any of them."

"You can't just leave that all behind."

"I don't have a real choice, do I? What is it called? A restraining order? If I fight it then I blow my life up here. My second chance."

"What do you mean?"

Joetta paused for a moment, she seemed to shift into a different head space. Her posture changed. The wife and mother, the alcoholic was gone, the broken pieces aligned and reformed before Belinda's eyes. Joetta willed herself to be what she used to be, not what she was.

"Banks is going to ask me to marry him."

Belinda didn't have to ask what Joetta would say to Bank's proposal.

"I supposed this was what your life was supposed to look like before Bruce Kelly walked up to us on this very beach."

"He broke up the Gulfside Girls." Joetta smiled, and Belinda took her hand. Joetta's smile was hollow. There was something dark behind her summer eyes now. Something that Belinda could never fix. "Look at that gorgeous sunset."

Belinda looked out to the sun, yellow with an orange ring around it. The clouds were white, and pink and then purple closer to the horizon. The sun dipped into the water.

"Quite a Grand Finale," Joetta said.

Belinda would help Joetta rebuild. Whatever it took, she would be there for her baby sister.

"Or maybe it's a beginning."

Somehow, they'd figure out a way to be there for Joetta's girls. Whether Bruce Kelly wanted them to or not.

Thirty-Five

DIDI
Present Day

Things were looking up. Ali had announced with little fanfare but with a firm commitment that she was going to stay and make a go of it at the Sea Turtle. Didi was overjoyed. It was an answer to a prayer.

She wanted this place to stay, to endure. She and Jorge had made so many memories for so many families, and now Ali would do the same.

Ali had every right to sell. And most would. But that soon-to-be ex-husband and the visit from Faye had helped Ali see what Didi had seen from the beginning.

Ali Harris was meant to be in this place at this time. Didi was so happy about it that she could barely stand it.

It had been nearly forty years since they'd made the offer to Bruce Kelly.

Didi thought back to the desperation she'd felt when her baby sister was thrown out of the girls' lives. They'd hatched a plan to sign this place over to the girls in hopes that it would entice Bruce. It didn't. Later she hoped they were building some sort of nest egg for the girls, or a college fund.

But Bruce had never let it be. Not once. And life had moved on.

Belinda Bennett had married Jorge Rivera, and he'd called her Didi from the start. A shortened from of Lindy, which guests at the country club had taken to calling her when she met Jorge.

Now, everyone called her Didi.

Seeing Ali made her heart ache and also leap with joy. This was that sweet little girl, all grown up, strong, beautiful, and the spitting image of Joetta.

When Faye showed up, Didi almost spilled the beans. It was all she could do, not to say it. Not to tell them everything.

But she'd stopped herself. How did you tell someone something that big? And would being honest mean she'd have to say goodbye to her nieces again? She'd barely gotten over it the last time; no chance she could do it twice.

Ali's arrival had come at the perfect time. Jorge and Didi could still do the work, but not as fast and not as well. Ali had shown them how she could bring the Sea Turtle roaring back to life. Her niece was supposed to be there, now and forever. It was more than she could ever dream of, but also more than she could reveal.

Didi was getting the linens from the washer to the dryer when Ali burst into the office.

"Did you know about this?"

"About?"

"I found out that the original owner of this place was Joetta Bennett. Joetta Bennet was my mother."

Didi looked at the papers that Ali had printed out. She knew full well what she was looking at. She knew full well when those papers were filed. And just who filed them.

All Didi had ever wanted was in front of her. The little girls she knew but left behind were here. Well, two of them had been. Bruce was no longer in their way. But how could Ali ever forgive her? How could Faye understand what they'd done? Didi blamed Bruce's cold stubbornness and Joetta's alcoholism, but she shared blame, too, in this secret.

Didi looked at the paper that transferred this property to the Kelly Sisters. From the Gulfside Girls to the Kelly Sisters. She knew exactly who owned this place then and now. She was the management company. Her delay tactics were exactly that.

When faced with the truth from Ali, Didi had lied. It was a lie she'd been telling for forty years, so it was easy to tell once more.

"No, never heard of that. But you know we've always just dealt with that P.O. Box, email, and management company, GG Properties."

She also knew exactly what GG Properties stood for. Gulfside Girl Properties. Over the years, she'd so hoped the Kelly Sisters would become the new Gulfside Girls. But it hadn't happened. She'd almost stopped hoping it would.

And then Ali had walked in. Bruce was no longer in their way.

Didi held her breath, and Ali looked back at the paper, walked around the desk, and sat down in the metal chair.

"My mom wanted us to have this. Did I tell you we found jewelry and vintage clothes? Didi, I always thought my mom was poor, you know? Or working class? But it looks like she was from here and had money."

Jorge walked into the middle of the conversation. Didi could see her husband was giving her a look. She decided she'd use him as a life preserver to get out of the ocean of history she was currently drowning in. She decided to run from this conversation as fast as her arthritic legs could take her.

"Oh, that's right, Jorge. Sorry Ali, we've got to get moving. Jorge is about to get sprung from his physical therapy appointment, and we don't want to miss this last one!"

She pretended she had no clue about Ali's history. About Joetta's. About her own. She was in very deep with her niece.

I can't lose her again!

"Oh, sure, yes, sorry." Ali was preoccupied with the revelation that her mother had left this property to her and her sisters. Rightly so. It was a bombshell for Ali, who'd been dealing with so many explosions in her life lately.

Didi wanted to tell her everything. And she would. But she needed time. Didi wanted Ali to stay. She didn't want the truth to send her running for the real estate agent. This was her only chance to make things right. And it was her only chance to save the Sea Turtle from the wrecking ball. Ali needed to stay. If she found out about the lie, Didi's lie, there'd be no way to keep her here.

Didi walked over to Ali and put a hand on her shoulder.

"Well, however it happened, this place is a magical gift. I'm so glad you're staying to help it flourish."

Ali looked up and covered Didi's hand with her own. "Me too."

Didi could have done it right then, spilled it all. But she didn't. Let it be this way for a little while longer.

"Okay, well. I better get this one to PT!" Didi turned and walked toward Jorge, who was glaring. She hoped Ali did not catch the fact that Jorge was clenching his jaw and willing Didi to confess.

"Happy graduation, Jorge!"

He nodded, and then Didi hustled him out of the office.

When they got out of earshot, Jorge grumbled at her. "I heard you lie. A bald-faced lie."

"Yes, shh."

"Why? She needs to know."

"Because I want her here, at least for now."

"Belinda Bennett Rivera, you're going to pay for this."

"I already have. I'll figure it out. Let's focus on you, okay?"

Didi ushered Jorge to their car and hoped her lie could hold just a little while longer while her niece made the Sea Turtle her home.

Ali had discovered who had owned the Sea Turtle before her. She'd discovered it was signed by her mother to the Kelly Sisters. But she didn't know the full story. She didn't know the half of it. Ali didn't know Didi's part in it. Or that secret was only the beginning.

Jorge got in the car, and Didi followed. She said a prayer for more time and some way out of the mess she'd helped manage.

Thirty-Six

ALI

"Okay, yes, I'll be on the lookout for those. It's 13 Gulfside Wayside Way, c/o Sea Turtle Building #1, Haven Beach, Florida."

The law firm of Michalak, Perna, and Janco had hammered out a good settlement. With the resort off the table, they'd agreed to Ted keeping the house, and Ali keeping her inheritance from Bruce. Ted kept his stupid car, too.

That meant Ali had some cash in the bank to live on while she did this crazy thing.

It was crazy right, in its way? Trying to make the Sea Turtle Resort work?

But she was doing it. Or trying, anyway.

Ali decided to inhabit Strawberry Hideaway Cottage for the time being. It was the smallest and furthest from the beach. She felt the best about occupying this space as the spring break crowd was about to descend. She had so much to do in the next few days to be ready for them.

She'd heard it was the make-or-break season for a Gulf vacation rental. According to the rental schedule calendar Didi handed over to her, they weren't fully booked. Ali saw it as a challenge. By this time next year, she'd have each cottage booked, and the entire Inn.

The list of things to do was long. At least the pool was looking better. Silvio, the pool guy, had started cleaning it out. And while there were repairs to make she felt good about the cottages. They were safe enough, clean enough, and well stocked.

The Inn was another story. That place was none of the above. The more she thought about that list, the longer it got. But one at a time, she'd knock it out; she'd make this place magical for every single guest.

Not that people were beating down the door yet. They had a long way to go to get fully booked. But this was the kind of challenge Ali lived for.

Faye had been right! Her little sister had been in the lead on this. She'd been the one to take charge and help Ali see a path forward. It was a good lesson for her to know it didn't always have to be her. Her sisters were grown, and she didn't have to be the mom all the time.

Faye had convinced Blair to give her a year. Blair needed the money the most. Ali felt guilty about that. Her first instinct was to care for Blair, not herself. But Faye pushed hard.

"Blair can give you this time. If Sea Turtle is a bust after a year? Two? We still own Gulfside property. We can sell and get the cash then."

Faye and Ali were working on a plan to appraise the true price of their mother's clothes. It seemed each dress was more valuable than the one before it. If Blair really needed cash, Ali would give Blair all the dresses and the jewelry to get her through.

She was worried about Blair, though. Her baby sister was going through something but hadn't shared what it was. Or was Blair the only sane one? Selling the Sea Turtle made more sense than staying. Except when you got here...and staying was all you wanted to do.

Ali was wrestling with her choice to stay. Every night, she weighed the consequences of hanging onto the Sea Turtle.

Was this selfish? Was it vindictive? Was she only doing this because Ted had pushed her to the edge?

Thankfully, Faye was her sounding board, and Faye believed Ali could do this. Didi did, too. And she wanted to do it.

From the moment she'd put her feet in the sand here at Haven Beach, she'd felt connected to it in a way she hadn't any other place.

Both her children had been ambivalent. They didn't know exactly what had happened between their father and their mother. Maybe that was okay. Dumping on the kids over the indiscretions and failure of the parents was selfish for certain. There was no debate in her mind on that. And eventually, her children would come here. It was impossible not to. It was paradise.

Ali walked down to the beach; she had purchased a beach cart for all the supplies. Tonight, it would be just the locals, her new friends, and the Riveras.

They had only days to go before the busy season on Haven Beach. Ali was terrified and excited about the onslaught of vacationers. She spent every day and night doing what she could to get ready. Each good experience she offered her guests, led to more guests. Unless they had a terrible time, then the reverse would happen. She needed to start out right with this season.

She had the cheese trays from Moe's and the wine she'd begun to source at an adorable winery up the coast, and she'd turned on the lights Henry had helped her string for the Hafners and Nobles. Forever the first guests she'd hosted here.

Ali was torn about the lights. Was that every night thing? Or only for special events? Ali eyed a future with beach weddings or retirement parties. This place has so much potential, and she had the background it make it happen.

But tonight, it was her new friends. She wanted them to see

how much she appreciated the warmth in which they had enfolded her. A stranger just one month ago. So the lights would twinkle!

Erica was the first to arrive. Her steal gray dreadlocks were tied with a ribbon in the back. She wore overalls, flip flops, and a look of gratitude that it was time to unwind with some vino.

"Oh, my gosh, I need this today! A tour bus showed up at noon!"

Ali handed her a glass.

And then, Patsy Gleaner appeared. Patsy had been momentarily crushed that Ali didn't want to put the place on the market. But the woman's quick wit, connections, and honesty had turned her into a fast friend.

"Girl, that's the most gorgeous kaftan I've ever seen!"

Faye had sent her the garment from their mom's stash. It felt strange but also magical to wear something of her mother's. Didi nearly cried when she saw it. Which was odd. Didi was being odd lately, but then again, there had been so many changes so quickly.

Henry showed up last. She kept looking for him, and finally, there he was.

She didn't know what was in store or how to feel about how happy it made her to see him.

Ali decided to keep that relationship in the friend zone. She wasn't ready for anything else. She also didn't trust her judgment. Ali had completely missed the fact that Ted was a serial cheater. Of all the upheaval she'd experienced in the last few weeks, that one had her questioning her own eyes. Her own senses. Had she always known? She didn't think so. But then how dumb was she to not see what had gone on under her nose?

Henry Hawkins was handsome, funny, tall, and oh so very Olyphant. But Ali wasn't ready for Olyphant level. No need to dive into the dating pool at the same time as she was learning to run this place.

Still, it was hard not to stare. He was so surfer cool as he added snacks from the Seashell Shack to the sunset smorgasbord she'd prepared.

"Whoa, not a cloud in the sky, gonna be a good one," Jorge said.

And Ali looked to the horizon.

The sun was flaming orange with deep fiery flares visible at the edges. The sky was pale blue, and the water gray.

How is it different every time?

"Grand Finale indeed," Ali whispered, she thought to herself.

"But new beginning too," Henry replied, and he clinked his glass with Ali's.

It was a new beginning. She was starting something brand new. With these new friends who'd quickly become family. And at her age? It was thrilling. And terrifying.

It was a haven, this beach.

And for now, it was hers.

The Gulfside Girls and Kelly Sisters Saga Continues in the next book of the Haven Beach Novels - Gulfside Inn

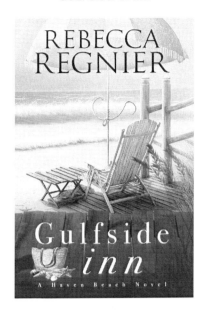

About the Author

Rebecca Regnier is an award-winning newspaper columnist, tv host, and former television news anchor. She lives in Michigan with her family and handsome dog. For all the latest from the beach and an exclusive bonus scene sign up for her newsletter or follow her on one of her socials. She loves to share laughs with her readers!

tiktok.com/@rebeccaregnier

facebook.com/rlregnier

instagram.com/rebeccaregnier

youtube.com/@RebeccaRegnierTV